Life as We Know It

Ma Vivek

I0672329

ISBN 978-0-9928533-6-5

Cover Design:
Ibrahim Rahman
http://www.ibrahimrahman.co.uk

Edited by Jan Andersen
http://www.creativecopywriter.org

PERFECT PUBLISHERS LTD
23 Maitland Avenue
Cambridge
CB4 1TA
England
http://www.perfectpublishers.co.uk

ii

Contents

Chapter	Title	Page
	Prologue	v
1	Hindsight in Sight for Carl	1
2	Stella Reflects on the Two Sides of a Coin	5
3	Carl Finds that Vulnerability Takes Courage	11
4	Stella is Dead Serious Before Life Takes Over	17
5	Carl Wants No Expectations and Gets the Unexpected	32
6	Stella Befriends Fears That Had Her Fooled	41
7	Carl Gives and Takes – or Perhaps Not	54
8	Stella Feels Incompatible with Herself.....................................	67
9	Carl Considers Concepts of Reality – or Maybe Relativity	82
10	Stella Spices Hot Topics	91
11	Carl Ends Up in a Mystery Where Ghosts May Not Be Such Ghastly Hosts	106
12	Stella is High on Life on the Ground	114
13	Carl Recalls the Call	123
14	Stella Discovers That No Reason Can Be Many Reasons	133
15	Carl Leaves the Corporate World to Incorporate Staying Open	140
16	Stella Playfully Reveals Her Passions	147
17	Carl Brings Up the Meaning of Life and Comes Down with Himself	155
18	Stella's Anger Management Leads the Way	161

19   Carl Touches a World Wide Web   171
20   Stella Trusts the Inner Critics Can Be
      Tamed   178
21   Carl Makes Do Without a
      Contingency Plan, and It is All Same
      Same, but Different   192
22   Stella's Hellish Pain Reminds Her of
      Heaven   205
23   Carl Figures Out That He Cannot
      Figure It Out, but Does So Anyway ..   214
24   Stella Strips a Long Story Short and
      Makes Her Debut   223
25   Carl Keeps His Real Estate Dreams
      and Stands His Ground with Stella ...   234
26   Stella in Her Way Advocates That
      Easy is Right, Right is Easy   242
      Epilogue   244
      Acknowledgements   247
      Appendix   249

Prologue

"You could always ask him what he really wants to do with his life."

As soon as I had popped the suggestion, I realised it was as valid for myself as it was for my friend's nephew. How come I so often tell others what I actually need to hear myself? And usually do not realise it, at least not until later. Moreover, asking the question is easy; giving it a little time to find some answers or directions has so far proven to be a major challenge.

I wonder why it is so difficult for so many of us to deal with the bigger issues in life, to look in, to acquaint ourselves with our deeper layers, instead of just clinging to the surface, to others' opinions, and maybe buy a new kitchen or car or cell-phone or handbag or something, in order to hopefully feel better for a moment or two? Nothing wrong with that; however, I do have a feeling that when I am lying there counting my last breaths, I probably will not say, "I wish I had worked more and earned more money, so I could have bought this and that and gone there and there..." Or perhaps I will? Who knows? What I do know is that I do not know much, and that I, at least sometimes, am willing to explore what findings might be there for me.

When I was a child I, like many others I guess, always thought that I would get a good education, a good job, meet someone, have a family, buy a house, throw parties, go on holidays to nice and sunny places - live a so-called normal, hopefully even successful (whatever that is) life - and at the same time I had the sense of not really fitting in, in general and also not into that. Thus, growing into my teens, a part of me started wondering, started feeling that I would not get there, that that ideal was for most people maybe, but for whatever reason not for me. Not having many clues as to what the alternatives were, I clung to the hope that I might get there anyway, if only I would be good enough, do well enough and do what was expected of me. However, it did not quite work out, at least not for the 'normal' life to happen. Then again, what is normal? What is normal for me is my normal, right? And what is normal for you is your normal. Hence, everything could be called normal, but maybe not average or mainstream.

I did what I could, got good grades and graduated, but found myself with basically no self-esteem or self-confidence in an economic recession. I found a flat, finally got a job that had at least some bearing to my education, fell in love with a handsome man, moved together, separated, felt as if I had lost the ticket to 'normal-hood', cracked into pieces and still held it together pretty well. There I was, a good citizen, employee, daughter, sister, aunt and friend, albeit not a very 'living' one; just surviving, day by day. I found some help to keep going by way of different kinds of psychotherapy – eventually acknowledging to myself that all those self-help books I had read over the years were insufficient for me in that situation, and reluctantly even took anti-depressants for some time.

Marriage, children, a job
And then a little snob
My dreams' and longings' goals
There are still just holes

All these dreams, expectations, frustrations and the bits and pieces of satisfaction that most of us have. I wrote those lines in my early twenties and perhaps some would say it still holds true, at least on the surface. And yet, something else is there; the haunting thought I always had that there must be more to life. Even if I had had all that, would I be content? To the extent that I know myself, I most likely would not. The longing for something else, something more, something imperishable, would probably still be there, was there, is there, and glimpses of that something else show me the direction, keep me going.

So here I am, with all the different parts and voices in me, telling me what to do and what not to do. I tend to criticise myself no matter what I do; including sharing this story with you, which has come to me about Carl and Stella - two people not really young anymore, not yet old, and busy with whatever many of us are busy with. It may not always be coherent; you may not always get what you think you want and you may make out of it whatever you want. A bit like life itself...

She loved him so much and he failed her
He loved her so much and she failed him
They believed they loved each other
Did they really?
Did they even know love?
Did they even know each other?
Did they even know themselves?

Chapter 1

Hindsight in Sight for Carl

What would you say
At the end of the day
If this is all there was
And you were not the boss
Yet the one on whom responsibility lay?

All; we were both longing for it all and seemed to be heading for nothing - nothing but destruction, at least with each other. So what else could I do? I had to leave Stella for both our sakes; that was what I convinced myself of. Admittedly, I did not handle it very well or nicely. Ending it with a phone call after almost eight years and having lived together – and, at least technically, still doing so – is not something that I am particularly proud of. I just heard myself finally say it. Looking back one could actually say that the ending somehow matched the beginning.

We met at work; both of us were part of a group of trainees beginning at about the same time in a subsidiary of one of these multinationals. It was actually a friendly group and, although one could perhaps have suspected the opposite, we all gave each other support and had a lot of fun, doing things together after work too. Stella and I soon let our eyes linger a bit longer on each other, giving the other little signs of attraction and appreciation, adding some extra spice also to our office hours.

1

Stella was maybe not what one might call a classical beauty, but still she had something that made her pretty and appear before my eyes, even when we were not seeing each other. To start with, her smile and glittering emerald green eyes, her soft and shining blond hair, which she had toughened up with a fairly short and wild hairstyle and the way she made me laugh and smile.

After working together for some time, there was a big party where some more action happened, but I was still not so sure about which way I wanted to go, even though things advanced between us. Not head over heels swept off my feet, but there was definitely something growing between us that had me hooked. There was also this other woman that I had not really been able to let go of, although nothing much had happened between us; or maybe rather, just because of that. Stella, of course, sensed this preoccupation – or whatever I ought to call it. Unfortunately, I had it confirmed by a fairly intimate message on a fax copy that was sent to me to the office from the other woman, and was lying around before I knew it had been sent to me. Stella made it clear that she would not be some second-best option and asked me to give the key to her flat back to her, and…well, we would still be colleagues. In a way, her anger and determination showed new sides to her, and a certain kind of aliveness and strength that I had not really seen before. I realised I wanted to keep the key. I wanted to continue with Stella.

Fairly soon, we moved in together, or to put it more precisely, I moved in with her. She had a really nice three-roomed flat and we thought we might start there since I only had a studio, and then see what the next move might be. We realised that moving in with someone is not so easy for either person, since one often feels he or she has to give up an already organised space, and the other feels he or she takes it, so after a while we decided to find a place that would be our mutual space from the beginning. We found and bought an old-style four-roomed flat and started renovating, step by step, room by room; throwing out linoleum flooring, whetting and oiling wooden floors, painting ceilings and walls and buying some new furniture. We had a good time together. We had fun, enjoyed each other; sex, cooking, renovating, movies, travelling and yet...after a while, there was something nagging.

As time went by, I got the feeling more frequently that I *wanted* it to be good more than I actually *felt* it was good. I wanted it to work; hence I told myself it *was* good, that Stella was the one for me - and in many ways she really was - pretending our life together was better than it was. It was as if trying to adjust into the relationship mould took the best of me, and thereby I also took the best of her. And I made her pay for my frustration. She did not deserve that, but I simply did not know how to deal with it, or talk about it for that matter. Thus I escaped, took a job in a town at a non-commuting distance, and ended up terminating the relationship in a phone call, obviously hoping she would accept it that way. And she did not really have any choice.

Of course, we had to see each other even though we did not work together any longer. We still had the apartment together, I had my things there and we still had to decide who would take what of the things we had bought together. And, we still had feelings for each other; there was still attraction despite my not being able to commit any more. It was not an easy time and more difficult than I had imagined to let go of her, to let 'us' go.

I started having second thoughts, even regretting almost that we had not had children together; having this idea that that could have made it easier, which I also told her. She asked me what the devil I was up to with that kind of torture. In further hindsight though, I can say that it was pure imagination or wishful thinking on my part. I have not yet known or heard of one single relationship where having children made it easier, my own included. Having children does add another dimension, that is for sure, but it is hardly a means to improve or save a relationship.

I did not realise it at the time, but in a way I guess you could say she was right and I was acting quite cruelly - and having had no clue is a pretty poor excuse.

Chapter 2

Stella Reflects on the Two Sides of a Coin

The new moon
So solid and frail
Touching my heart
Always there
Close yet far away

At first, Carl for some reason did not really catch my attention. Not that he was not good-looking in some sense; quite tall and fit, sun-bleached, softly curled hair, beautiful sensitive hands and quite male in his energy, but it was as if we could not really connect. Actually, I cannot say what changed that, but apparently something did. Hence, it was not love at first sight, but as days became weeks and weeks became months, the attraction grew and I fell deeply, truly, madly in love like never before, and maybe never after, since existence never repeats itself, although they do say history does.

The exhilaration I felt when I discovered that he had left some of his things in my flat – that meant he would come back...and stay on! I think I was blushing there in my solitude. We, or rather he, had been a little back and forth; I could sense a certain hesitation during the first months of dating and hanging out together, but leaving his things behind was a good sign. And we kept going for a while. Then that fax came from an ex-, or whatever, girlfriend, saying something about him coming to visit her. I just marched into his room at work and dropped it on his desk.

"I believe this is for you."

No doubt I said that in a quite cold and harsh way, even though burning inside, then turned around, went out and continued to my room, in turmoil. I guess blushing again, however this time for a completely different reason.

I did some intense workout in the early evenings for a couple of days; a kind of catharsis I would say looking back. He then wanted to see me, wanted to talk. I agreed to that if it could be somewhere neutral. A cup of coffee after work, in a nearby café that we usually just passed by, apparently felt safe enough to both of us. Sitting in front of him, trying to stay collected and cool, letting my eyes wander and discover the art deco decorations on the walls on the upper floor of that old-fashioned classical place, the whole situation seemed surreal.

Our eyes finally met for a moment and I guess the situation felt as awkward to him as it did to me. Carl cleared his throat and somewhat formally thanked me for coming. I asked him what he wanted to talk about, what there was to say. He looked down at the marble top of the table. I could see him taking a deep breath, before saying that he had not been clear to any of us, least of all to himself, because he had not been sure where things – his feelings – were heading with her and me. I was angry, hurt and sad. I told him that I would not be his doormat and asked for my key back – which I did not get, because he claimed that he did not have it with him. Bullshit.

Sometime later, there was another big celebration and party and I was definitely not going to let Carl stop me from having fun. Towards the end of that night, he wanted me to come with him, to leave when he did and go to his place, or mine. I told him I would not do that and instead I stayed on dancing. Early the following morning, he called and said he had talked to the 'ex' and told her he had fallen in love with someone else, that he had met a new girlfriend and that he wanted to be with her; that is with me.

"And how am I supposed to trust you?"

I was, of course, not convinced.

"I don't know... I guess you just will have to... I'm sorry. I miss you. I love you."

I was still very much in love with him and wanted 'us' to happen, so I melted. We started over; he moved in, we moved, made plans and enjoyed life. In spite of it all, something was not as smooth as I would have wished it to be. More than once, I ended up apologising for something unnecessarily in order to try to make him feel better again and ease the atmosphere. More than once, I ended up making excuses to myself for him not behaving like I would have pictured a loving partner to behave. And, more often than not, I was just like putty in his hands, doing anything to make him happy and keep him happy, feeling so lucky to be with him.

One late afternoon, being the first to come home, I looked around in the flat and thought about our ideas of how to make it more *our* place; what colours to paint the walls in the rooms that still needed decorating, the new wallpapers we had looked at and how to fix the floors, wanting to make it lighter, yet cosy. We had already finished with the kitchen, bathroom and our bedroom. Then I noticed the answering machine was blinking, so I pressed the play button and heard a voice offering him a job some 500 km away.

Fax messages, voice messages; I hated those darned machines and messages! What the heck was that all about? I became cold and warm simultaneously. First I sat down, played the message a couple of times more, as if I could not believe what I had just heard, looked around again and wondered if it was all a bad joke, like Candid Camera or something. Then I started cleaning, watering the plants and doing the laundry; anything to keep myself busy and not explode inside.

Confronted when he came home, Carl's explanation and excuse was that he had not wanted to unnecessarily stir things up before he knew he was offered the job, but yes, it was a very good opportunity, he wanted to move and go for it, and if I wanted to move too, that would be great. If I wanted to move too?! I so much wanted to believe him – in us – that of course I wanted to go with him.

He accepted the offer after some negotiating and moved, while I stayed on and started applying for jobs in the new town. Then, when I had one opening presented, he closed the door in my face in a phone call; one I will never forget.

Incredulity followed by an immediate, immobilising, physical pain. Everything became black and it felt as if I could not breathe. It was as if he had stabbed me with a knife in the stomach, or in the back, or both. I do not know how, but I managed to call a very dear friend who came over. I also managed to go to work the next morning, VERY early. When my neighbouring colleague showed up, greeted me and asked how I was doing, I just burst into tears and there was not much else to do than to go home to that empty apartment, our apartment, after having written a note to my boss that I was sick.

When I returned to the office the next day, there was a rumour, somewhat ironically, that I was pregnant. Well, I was not; it felt rather like the opposite and I admit to having had difficulties with appreciating that irony.

Life takes its turns. At the time, I was really devastated by this one. But then again, with a little distance, I would say that I am happy to have had what we had and also for what came out of our separation. I finally swallowed some of my pride, left the self-help books at least partly aside and sought some support from a counsellor, who helped me to find ways to keep my head above water. Step by step, I started enjoying life again, with or without a significant other.

I am probably not the only one, but much as I might want things to be different, might wish to be continuously on a high; in order to get the rush of the peaks, the dark pits have their place too. Without the lows there would be no highs, just a flat-line, and most of us know what that means: no sign of life. If we had our favourite food every day, for example, then we would probably get tired of it and, moreover, we would suffer from malnutrition, no matter how healthy the chosen food might be. We need variety.

If and when we can allow it to be, life is such a ride; if we just go with the flow, there is so much beauty in it all. Blissful moments are there with all their wonders, as are other moments, which at first might feel less blissful, with much pain and even desperation. Still, having experienced bliss somehow makes the desperate moments bearable, adds another quality to them. Looking back, they might actually even be blissful in their way; polarities that need each other, define each other, fade into each other. One cannot exist without the other; thus we cannot choose or repress one without repressing the other.

A challenge for many of us, at least for me, might be to stay open to all feelings and emotions, even the so-called negative ones; to relax with these polarities, staying anchored in the middle, instead of struggling or trying to choose sides. They too are a gift, offering a wide range of possibilities and experiences. It is a learning to accept what is there and thereby find an inner distance and peace, while also acknowledging the longing for something else that sometimes surges, together with the part in me that actually enjoys life the way it is, in this body the way it is. After all, sometimes I do see it; I have and am all of it, but there is also a space in me where I am none of it. Somewhere, I am weightless, shapeless, warm and cool, transparent white and sparkling with colour, ecstatic and peaceful, empty yet full, everything and nothing…as are all of us. And then change, change, change.

It came to me one night whilst looking at the beautiful, shining – or reflecting – half-moon, that we are so much like it. Sometimes we are all light, sometimes all dark, sometimes half and half, or something in between, and always changing from the one to the other. It is as though we move on a pendulum, which intrinsically cannot remain in one position. It feels as though it moves in a regulated way that we can handle, as long as we do not get in the way of ourselves and want to have it otherwise. It is like the proverb: "It is always darkest just before dawn."

Chapter 3

Carl Finds that Vulnerability Takes Courage

What to do?
Where to go?
I just don't know
Nothing to do
Nowhere to go
Staying with what is
Digging deep
Rising high
Al(l)one

So there I was; free, with a new job in a new town, a 'new', but same old me, still pretending we might get back together. That made me feel better, as I believed that would make Stella feel better, only that last part I did not see. I did not have much idea about anything; or maybe it was actually the opposite, that I had a lot of ideas and beliefs, but not so much clarity. I thought I just needed time and space, and took it, acting like a real coward in the way that I did it.

I kept telling myself that the man whom I was really needed to break free, break up, take that space, and I felt very male about it. Talking about fooling myself; what I saw later was that I was not man enough to face reality as it was, to deal with whatever issues we had in a constructive way, to stand up for my needs, to meet hers, and instead sneaked away. I thought I was strong and action-oriented, when in fact I was running away like a chicken.

To act differently, to stay and give us a chance to work things out, to maybe even allow myself to feel vulnerable, probably would have meant that I would have to be in touch with my real feelings. How afraid I actually was of committing to the relationship, of having children, of ending up – what I would consider to be – stuck. To see and to feel these fears and then take action towards what I really wanted, would have taken courage, which I did not have.

I did not think I was afraid of anything. If I'm not afraid, then I do not need courage. I just do whatever it is I am about to do. When fear is there, then courage is needed to take the risk of doing that which scares me, because I can see that the desired outcome will be worth the risk, worth moving myself through the fear. Courage leads the way to feel the fear and do it anyway. I read somewhere that the linguistic root of the word 'courage' is 'cor', the Latin word for heart and also the Old French word 'corage', meaning heart, innermost feelings, temper. Courage stems from the heart. When I got to know this, I could see it.

Usually when I do something that seems scary or risky and courage is needed, it is my thoughts that keep bugging me about the dangers. Deep down – in my heart – I just know I need or want to do it, and find a way to go through with it. Something good always comes out of it, even if some, including the voices inside, would say I failed. In a way, I could not really fail, since at least I tried. But with Stella, I bailed out. I slowly realised that despite my changing 'everything', I was still there, doing pretty much the same as I had always done. Wherever I go I bring myself.

For a significant time, I really tried to have my cake and eat it too, as the saying goes. I was enjoying my new-found freedom and at the same time trying to keep Stella on the hook, in case I eventually realised that I did want her after all. Of course, in the long run, this did not work for either of us.

I would never have guessed what life had in store for us. Chances are that if someone had asked me, I probably would have said that she was just someone I used to know. As big an understatement as that would have been, I would rather have stuck to that than answer any other potential questions or enquiries about her, or us; the things we do, or would have done, in this case.

I have realised that I often have this inclination to belittle what is actually important, and instead make a mountain out of a molehill. Luckily, with Stella, things turned out differently, albeit much later. I connected with her again, after many years, and she became someone I keep getting to know. Along the way, I also discover more about myself, with our talks being a source of inspiration and exploration, making me feel and think about things to which I may not have given much attention otherwise.

"Do you think one can be consciously unconscious? And to me, unconscious and subconscious, the way we talk about it are basically the same thing."

I simply had to ask her, since it had been on my mind for some time already.

"Ok, fine with me. Still, how do you mean?"

"Well...I think I mean that sometimes you choose to be unconscious; that it can be like a conscious choice."

"Like taking a break from our usual full-on consciousness you mean?" Stella smiled.

"Yeah, something like that." I couldn't help but laugh. "It can be quite exhausting, you know."

"Ha, ha. No, I wish I did."

The way we both found it so funny was probably a clue.

"Break or not, what would you say?" I wondered.

"Give me an example. Since you asked, you must have thought of something."

"Err...ok; like when you allow yourself to get drunk, or a bit tipsy, while enjoying a couple of glasses of fine wine together with, say, some cheese, or other complementary food?"

"And the enjoyment of sipping the wine lasts longer than the food?"

"Right."

"Well Carl, I'd say that many of us would probably like that as an option."

"Why do I sense a 'but' coming up?" I sighed loudly.

"Yeah, why do you?" Stella smiled again. "And here it comes: but, I'd say that's more likely to be another trick of the mind; perhaps we could call it our human conscious unconscious – for today anyway."

"Yes! There you go!"

"Now you wish..."

"I do, I do, but please!"

"In my experience at least, a part of the mind has this tendency to want to be good and to do good in some sense, whatever that good is, and if being conscious has been identified as a goal or something desirable or however one calls it, then the mind wants to find itself there."

"Aha?"

"Well, as I understand it, and I might be wrong of course, but if you're really conscious and aware of your actions, then you will not, or cannot, do something unconscious, either to yourself or to others of course. Drinking too much might be a conscious decision, but the act as such, with its effects, is basically unconscious, no matter how we look at it, since we gradually lose whatever alertness we may have and we know it's not good for the body, even though initially it might be pleasurable to the taste buds and our mood." Stella looked at me with glittering eyes.

"Like I said, exhausting."

"Yeah, I guess it can be as long as there is effort and trying, and not the natural state of being."

"Well, like they say, maybe in the next life. In the meantime, I guess we all have to bear with ourselves and all our conscious unconsciousness and unconscious consciousness and also those who don't seem to bear with us." I could not help but wonder where that one came from.

"On that note, thank you for bearing with me!"

"Likewise."

"And I will probably still have that tasty extra glass sometimes."

I actually could not even imagine not doing so.

"Uhum, me too. By the way, can you recommend a wine to go with a chicken and pistachio dish? I'm going to make it for some friends who are coming over on Friday and it would be fun to try something new."

Bearing with each other was no longer the question. Remembering that little discussion and others that we have had, it feels like our friendship has become... maybe stimulating could be one label. Friendship with her was not at all something I pictured when we broke up. Or, to be more accurate, when I broke up with her. Fortunately, something proved me wrong.

We meet, talk, discuss all kinds of topics, and it is not about being right or wrong, or convincing the other. As it happens, it is more as though we broaden our perspectives and maybe deepen them too. Above all, we enjoy embroidering on the fabric of life.

Chapter 4

Stella is Dead Serious Before Life Takes Over

We just have no idea do we
This life is given to you and to me
And the night is so beautiful and light
This time so promising and bright
So how can it be
A friend I will never again see
Is so much here with me
Oh beloved ray of light
It is a good time for your flight

After initially feeling that life ended with that separation, things gradually changed. Under the cloud of despair, I allocated myself a number of years to get back into mainstream life with a new man, a successful career, a nice apartment or house and, hopefully, children. If that did not happen before a certain time, I would take measures to put an end to this, what I considered, pointless life. When the stated time came closer, something else in me apparently grew stronger, and one day I found myself thinking that 'The End', or 'death', in some sense had already happened; that the death of the relationship with Carl actually presented the opportunity for something new to take place. So I did take measures to end the meaningless life, just not in the way I had it figured out.

17

Having tried all kinds of traditional therapy, my longing and curiosity led me to what I could call complementary forms too. I discovered meditation and more specifically the active meditations created by the Indian mystic or enlightened man Osho, and his proposed ways of combining western therapy with meditation.

I still remember the feeling I had when I first read one of his books, which are transcriptions of discourses from him. I was turning the pages with amazement and wonder; here was someone who somehow talked right to me – and from me. It was new, but well-known at the same time, giving me a feeling of excitement, of being almost overwhelmed and yet so relaxed by having found him, reading his words and – almost strangely since I had not met him – feeling a strong connection from the heart. It was something – someone – I wanted to explore more of.

Osho also realised that modern man, and westerners in particular, have suppressed so many feelings that need to be dealt with and expressed in a safe way, before they can actually sit with some detachment from their busy minds. And I did; express a lot of things, that is, especially in therapy groups with breathing exercises and in some of the active meditations – I still do occasionally. More than once I surprised myself with how much I had obviously been carrying around in terms of anger and sadness, but behind them there was also strength, joy, relaxation and love. With the breathings and the meditations, it was as if my inner control tower could have a break; I could let go and get in touch with what was actually there, in me, get to know more of me. It was all mind-blowing and things just got better and better. I might not really have wanted to die, but for quite some time I had certainly not been very keen on living. Now, life was exciting most of the time and I could feel a curiosity about what turns it might take.

Out of the blue one day, some 15 years after we split up, Carl contacted me and a new kind of connection between us started growing unexpectedly. I think this was a surprise to both of us. It turned out that we lived in the same town again and the fact that for years we had not even bumped into each other, or heard of each other, was rather astonishing too. In that conversation, we agreed it would be fun to meet, hence we decided to do so. After the first reunion, we continued seeing each other regularly, usually over a cup of coffee or two. We both gave priority to this; I assume since we both felt we gained a lot from each other. Our unplanned subjects, and pointless talks could be about life, death, fashion, food, travelling and big issues as well as small; anything in fact, but usually with a quality of exploring and surprise, which I enjoyed a lot. In between, I noticed myself taking mental notes of things that flashed by, or popped up, or lingered and which I would like to talk to Carl about.

"I don't know; I just cannot help but think it's such a waste."

"Ok, help me out here. What is a waste and why?"

Carl looked at me curiously.

"A friend of mine all of a sudden sank down to the floor and died on the spot last week. It was probably an aneurysm that burst."

I swallowed, feeling tears knocking on the door. It was still unreal to me and difficult to grasp.

"Oh, I'm sorry. Someone close?" Carl asked, concerned.

"Yeah, he was in a way very close, even though we didn't see each other that often, but whenever we connected it felt easy and warm. A part of me thinks it's such a waste because he meant so much to so many people and he had so much more to give and share. It just feels too early."

I could feel myself looking at Carl as if I wanted him to give me an explanation or a reason, and he seemed to sense that.

"Well, what can I say? I have a feeling though that when death happens suddenly, we usually tend to think it is a waste. But what do we know? I mean, as shocking as it might be to those around, as tragic and untimely as we might think it is, apparently it was his time to go. I guess this may sound hard to some - and of course it is easier to say when you haven't been close - but maybe he was spared from something. It sounds as though he had had a good life, and a death presumably fast enough not to feel pain and suffer. That's the way I would like to go if I could choose."

Carl looked at me a little hesitantly and I looked back at him, feeling a little surprised by his frankness and sincerity.

"I agree; me too. I just miss him, and I guess I'm angry and sad about not getting more of him. At the same time, I am so incredibly grateful to have met him, to have had and have him in my life, for all that he gave and shared."

There was a little pause, as if an angel had walked through the room.

"And you can still have him, as much as you want in a way."

"How do you mean?"

"Well, he is not here physically anymore, but no one can take away what you had with him and you can always go back to that, even talk to him should you wish. He is one of your treasures, no longer in the outer, but for sure still in the inner. And unless you make him your only friend or speaking partner, I don't think anyone is going to think that you're crazy," Carl said softly. He smiled and looked at me.

"Luckily I have you too…and a few more."

I thought about the friends that are such an important part of my life and managed a smile back.

"You do. Speaking of life and death and thoughts of waste, if you don't mind my broadening the subject, I think I have another aspect; that of coping with the death of a loved one, such as a lifelong partner."

Carl paused, which I felt as an invitation to either encourage him or change direction.

"Ok?" I wanted him to continue.

"Like I said, if you don't mind, and I don't know why this comes to me, now that you've told me about your friend, but maybe there's a grief I haven't dealt with. Now I can, and hopefully this can support, or be a part of your grieving too?"

"It's fine with me. Maybe you're right on both counts."

"Thank you."

Carl gave me an almost shy, boyish smile and continued.

"Of course, there is no way I can even imagine how it would be to lose a partner after decades together. I mean, after such a long time, it is more or less inevitable that you become closely knit. The other becomes an intrinsic part of your life."

21

"Yes, it's almost funny sometimes; you should have seen my ex's parents."

It was strange; I had thought about neither that boyfriend nor his parents for a long time.

"They bickered and even fought almost every day. If they didn't see each other because of work or whatever, then arguing and nagging on the phone would do. According to my boyfriend, they had done so for the last 40 or so years. Then, when his father died suddenly, I would have expected some relief for his mother after the initial shock, but it was as though she was totally lost without him. The fighting and arguing had become her fuel."

"Yes, it really is amazing how most of us so often seem to cling on to whatever is there to cling on to; bad relationships, boring jobs, our misery. Somehow, we seem to want to fight with life or a partner, even after he or she is dead."

Carl shook his head slowly.

"It is, and maybe not. I mean, it is familiar; we think we know what to expect and what is expected from us and thus it's quite comfortable and safe in a way, even if it is perceived as bad or boring. If we really analyse what we get from it, it is apparently worth something, otherwise we would probably walk away from it."

At least that was the conclusion I had reached.

"Maybe the experts are right after all." Carl smiled. "Maybe our inner child runs the show and on some level makes our partner our parent, someone we expect to fulfil our unfulfilled needs, so we test them, challenge them and provoke them and do all kinds of things, usually without realising of course."

"Yes, very likely, and maybe it's what we unconsciously hope for rather than what we actually get that makes us feel so lost when the other is gone. Then the hope is lost too, until we realise that we are adults and can look for what we want with many others, in many different ways and places."

"That sounds reasonable, at least in theory."

Carl nodded, blinked, and continued.

"And coming back to the loss of that long-time partner dilemma, I know someone who, since his wife's death, has almost stopped living. He locks himself in, in what used to be their house, and spends most of his days watching TV. He prefers not to see his friends - with the occasional exception of another widower, and almost reluctantly his children and grandchildren. Naturally, they feel as though they have not only lost their mother and grandmother, but also their father and grandfather. In my world, that is a waste of life and maybe of friendship, since I am selfish enough to feel I lost a dear friend and mentor."

"Yes, maybe it is, maybe it isn't. I mean, it's so easy to have opinions about how others live, or should live their lives, instead of taking responsibility for our own. And like you said before, what do we know, really? Except that once someone or something is born, death is bound to happen sooner or later, and we all have our different lots in life. The bottom line is, I guess, that we all basically do the best we can in any given situation, depending on where we're at. Ideally, we can only lovingly respect each other and how we choose to live our lives, or deal with our grief and whatever, while we're here."

I stopped, realising that what started out as personal had become rather general in some sense.

"And we never know how we'll react in a certain situation until we're there, in it. Considering how emotional I get sometimes just saying goodbye to a beloved friend I don't see that often, or in some separations..." I looked at Carl and smiled before I continued. "...I just wonder how I might have reacted after a long relationship."

For a moment, silence prevailed. I noticed my thoughts reflecting on our ponderings.

"This afternoon has taken its turns. Are we becoming technical or something here, because we don't really want to feel and get involved, or are we just getting in touch with a healthy distance?"

I obviously needed to give air to my observation.

"Hmm, well, I'd go with the healthy distance – and facts of life. You know, the only two things we know about life are, like you said – that we're going to die one day, having absolutely no idea when and secretly believing we'll be the exception to the rule, yet sometimes reminded about how fragile life actually is. Still, we have this tendency to forget that and take it for granted, and on the way we're going to pay taxes."

Carl sounded almost pleased with having remembered these facts that many of us often try to ignore.

"For sure; and not knowing what the journey will look like is also what adds spice and value to it, isn't it?"

This was something I had to remind myself of every now and then.

"It is. How exciting would it be if we knew about all the twists and turns? Although I have to admit I would have wanted to know at least some answers, especially when life has been difficult to cope with.

24

But then again, I guess that implies that I would like to have 'positive' answers, otherwise I would have been inclined to put myself six feet under."

Carl finished his coffee before he carried on.

"Like the old saying, 'as long as there's life there's hope'. I'm sorry if I'm overly worldly, but at this very moment I hope for some more coffee. Would you like some too?"

"Yes, please."

He went to get refills, while I waited for him to come back.

"Thank you." I took my cup.

"You're welcome. Where were we? Ah yes, hope."

Carl put his cup on the table and sat down again. I continued.

"Yes. So, one could say that not knowing is basically what keeps us going and life is quite exciting and even adventurous if we let it be, or rather, no matter what."

"Even without climbing mountains, or travelling all over the planet, or driving too fast, or changing partners, or whatever kicks we might be looking for in the outer? I mean, we have no idea what the next moment will bring, really."

As he said this, something in Carl seemed, almost reluctantly, to relax and he sighed as he leaned back.

"Right, we don't and that's where we started today, isn't it? We might tend to forget this and think we do, but that is a full on illusion when you think about it."

I looked at Carl.

"I imagine this could be good news if you're in a so-called bad situation, and maybe less good news if you're in what we might call a good situation or, hmm, what you perceive as good or bad." He smiled.

"Ha, ha, yes, could be. And also knowing that there is an end to everything; we simply don't know how and when, and the paradox that the only constant thing in life is change. Just look at the two of us."

"Indeed, and so many of us so often walk around saying that nothing happens in our lives."

Carl laughed and pointed to himself. "Touché!"

"Well, some inevitable changes we may just not want to see, like our bodies getting older and changing – and some of us, not me included I might add, do our very best to keep the body fit and even use surgery to keep the illusion of staying young. In that way we are trying to defy ageing and death."

"Well that, Stella, I'd say, is one splendid example of wishful thinking, but it does create a certain number of jobs."

The economist and business owner in Carl was fuelled.

"Mmm, if we consider the beauty industry in a broad sense, we're probably talking about a turnover of billions."

"Yes, and correct me if I'm wrong Stella, but it seems to me as if women are over-represented in these markets."

"I'm afraid you're right and I wonder why it's like that? I don't know how many times it has struck me when I've read interviews or articles about people; there are nearly always comments about the look and clothing if it is about a woman, but hardly ever if it is about a man."

This was something I had first noticed when I was in school, a lifetime ago.

"I haven't really thought about it, but I do take your word. We men also are lucky to benefit from the so-called charm of the grey temples." Carl stroke his temples, as grey as they were these days. "Never heard that about a woman, as far as I can remember."

"No, me neither. Speaking for myself, when I was a teenager and had anorexia, I told myself that in the beginning I wanted to lose weight to become slimmer and more attractive, but then it got out of hand and I looked sick more than anything. There are undoubtedly a number of other reasons too for my getting into that state, which we need not go into now. Later on in life, I was saying that I couldn't understand how women could buy into the hunt for different, expensive face creams etc., yet when I could afford them, I found myself buying into that too. Maybe not the most expensive ones, but pricey enough."

I shook my head.

"Ha, ha, yes, you do have beautiful skin!" Carl leaned over and touched my face with his hand. "And very soft too!"

"Yeah right; the benefits of affordable luxury. I'm surprised I haven't been headhunted for their ads."

"They don't know what they're missing!"

"The thing is that I, and I believe I could say we, have been so indoctrinated that it actually feels a lot better to put on my Clarins, or Clinique, or Origins, or Lancôme, or whatever cream, rather than one from L'Oréal, or Nivea, or something else from the supermarket."

"Now you've lost me." Carl looked amused.

"Good! I'm happy. But they are working hard on getting you men too. From a business point of view, I suppose that's inevitable. Of course, they wouldn't settle with half the market."

"So, where does all this leave us? Your favourite brand recommendation, or our starting an anti-beauty movement?"

"Probably neither, but possibly. Or at least an anti-artificial beauty movement and an appreciation of the natural beauty, which is always there if we really look."

I looked around and pointed to the one flower in a small vase on the table.

"Look from another space or perspective than that of the media and ads, you mean?"

"Yes, exactly, looking from the embracing heart rather than our judgmental minds. Easier said than done, but at least we can make the effort, step by step."

My fingers did a little walk across the table.

"We will have caused more unemployment and the disappearance of the vanity industry." Carl smiled.

"That will be the day."

"Yes, I wouldn't worry about that, but it is sad, isn't it?"

Carl motioned his head towards a table by the entrance, where some girls in their early teens with heavy makeup and quite revealing clothes were sitting.

"What?"

"The way even teenagers, and particularly girls like them for instance, seem to be under such immense pressure to look a certain way, according to ideal body shapes that don't often exist naturally. Many models have had themselves fixed and most pictures, ad clips and movies have been photoshopped or otherwise manipulated."

"Yes, I agree, it's very sad. And it seems to be getting worse. Today, you even find teenage girls who have had their lips or cheeks fixed with Botox or

28

Restylane, or something similar, and their breasts filled with silicone implants."

I shook my head to emphasise the incredulity of where we're heading, or where we already are.

"Who knows where we're ending up. Another thing I heard about is doctors prescribing anti-depressants to 12 to 13-year-old children. That's preposterous. As a father I get scared."

Carl looked at me solemnly.

"It's horrific if you ask me. It is as if we cannot allow anyone to be a bit low or sad for a while, which is unavoidable, not least in puberty, and the thing is that if we can't allow that, we also do not allow joy and happiness, since that's the other side of the coin."

"Welcome to limbo land."

"I'm just so glad that I feel I can say, 'I'm out of there!' At least generally."

"Me too, and I promise you I will do my very best to keep the children out of limbo and in themselves, in life, a roller-coaster as it may be."

Carl symbolically hit his fist on the table.

"You'd better Carl, or I'll be on your back!"

"I presume my neck will need some special attention then, since keeping the children out of limbo and in life will inevitably make me frustrated and annoyed at times, thinking they are a pain in the neck – or I'll have you there."

In spite of what he just predicted, Carl looked remarkably happy.

"Ha, ha! No gain without pain; you know that!"

That afternoon had been full of twists and turns. Even thinking about it made me lightheaded, so coming out in the street again I looked around, walked a few steps, stopped and leaned against a lamppost and closed my eyes. I breathed deeply and attempted to collect and ground myself a bit more, thinking a tree would have been nicer, but this was city life. We had touched on some heavy subjects, and our conclusion had been to live and enjoy life with its ups and downs as much as we can, while we can. I remembered having heard somewhere, that there is more life in life when death is around. Carl also had reminded me about something I had written to him when his cousin died in an accident:

Dear Death,
You are there
The time will come
I don't know where, or how, or when
I may say 'if' and 'then'
Still, you tell me
That here now
Life is
Thank you

My friend appeared before me, smiled and faded away. I would miss his physical presence; how could I not? But like Carl said, I would in some sense still have him.

I opened my eyes again. The sky was clear and blue and in front of me the city's rather grand old castle was enthroning, with its towers in all four corners and the river surrounding it. There is so much beauty around. Indeed, we all have our history and destiny. I could feel the gratitude for getting to know mine and for all the friends I had met on the journey so far. Not only do we all have our own history, we also carry the history of our ancestors, affecting us in different ways whether we realise it or not. Yet, more important than that is what history we create here now; what imprint we want to leave behind. We need to ask or remind ourselves how we can contribute towards making this world a better, more loving and more sustainable place; starting with ourselves and our actions.

A mother and child passed and the little boy smiled and waved to me. I smiled and waved back and felt that it was a good moment to move on.

Chapter 5

Carl Wants No Expectations and Gets the Unexpected

If I were me
Then who would I be?
Who am I?
Does it matter?
I am me

Walking out of the office to meet Stella that day felt like a reward. When the door closed behind me I instinctively took a deep breath of relief, or maybe it was relaxation. I had time, so I decided to walk there. I could take the bus home later instead of the car, or I could walk back and get the car. Realising what issues preoccupied me, I laughed out loud, since it felt like such a shift from earlier. I noticed some people looking at me with suspicion, which made the situation even funnier. Entering the café, I was still in a surprisingly good mood and Stella was already there, waiting for me and checking what the place had to offer.

"Hi Stella; I'm so happy to see you today!"
I really was, since I had had one of *those* days at work.
"Hi Carl! That sounds good to me. How about all the other days?"
Stella smiled as she turned towards me and we hugged.

"Then too, but today I really need to be somewhere where there are no expectations, either from you or me." Or from anyone else for that matter, I thought to myself.

"And you call that no expectations?" Stella laughed.

"Ah yes, you got me there. Nothing like a good old contradiction in terms, right?"

I hugged her again, kissed her cheek, before going to get our coffee and a table.

"Well, what's up? How come this aversion to expectations today?" Stella asked.

"I'm beginning to think that aversion might spread to other days too."

I exaggerated a little, but no smoke without a fire, as they say.

"Now I'm curious."

Stella loosened the foam of the cappuccino by making a circle with the spoon along the inside rim of the cup.

"It's just that expectations almost inevitably lead to disappointment, but seem nevertheless unavoidable and inbuilt in our psyches."

I sighed and wondered where that good mood had gone. Knowing these Wednesdays with Stella, I was however confident it would come back before too long.

"I agree. What happened today?"

"Just one of these almost everyday situations at work, which this morning turned out to threaten a major new contract. It could also have been at home of course, but since I left very early, that particular one has not yet happened today."

"And?" Stella insisted.

"Well, you know, you expect someone to do a certain thing according to how and when you've agreed, and when that doesn't happen..." I let the words fade away.

"It must have been something important and someone you usually think you can count on."

Stella took a sip of her coffee, which apparently had reached a drinkable temperature, since she did not want it so hot. She seemed to enjoy it, put the cup down and looked at me.

"Yes! Why do you say that by the way?" I wondered.

"Because you're so upset. Otherwise, like you say, we constantly have expectations that aren't met and we hardly even think of it. Unless it's something you consider important and someone you consider trustworthy or important. At least that's my experience."

"Yeah...and, when it falls back on yourself it's kind of annoying."

I was not sure whether I was angry because I felt let down, or because it created additional, unforeseen work to do, which was bad enough in that already stressful situation.

"What did you do? Did you get through the challenges?"

"Yes, I think I did. It looks like we're on track again with the deal. It took some extra energy though and maybe bruised some egos, but it boosted others' too, I guess."

"Yours too?" She looked at me with the hint of a teasing smile.

"Ha, ha, yes, in both ways I'd say."

"Please tell me; this sounds interesting."

Stella's interest somehow made me feel better. They do say that we men love to talk about ourselves. At this thought I felt an internal smile growing.

"I bet. Ok, the bruise..." I hesitated a moment. "I suppose I was hurt and didn't feel respected when the job hadn't been done by someone I trusted, so I had to do it myself. Not completing it within the agreed time, wouldn't have been to my advantage with the client. The boost; well, at the meeting with the client, I received some positive feedback, which I admit to taking pride in, and I flattered myself with being THE reliable and efficient one in the office...kind of." I stopped.

"That's honest – and apparently true. At least today." Stella smiled.

"Ha, ha, yes; who knows about tomorrow?"

Laughing about it eased some of the tension I had felt inside.

"Yes, who knows? What is also kind of funny is how little we know, even about ourselves."

Stella seemed to be making some associations.

"How do you mean?"

"Well, I've heard and read that 95-99% of what we do is controlled by our unconscious and certainly our egos, superegos and expectations play under those terms too; as does the one you thought you could rely on."

"Probably. But you say up to 99% out of the unconscious? That's almost scary. It's like we're walking around like icebergs and all we see are the tips. It's not so strange that we have this tendency to bump into each other so often without really understanding why," I said, flabbergasted, while trying to absorb what she had said.

35

"I like that image with the icebergs. Maybe we can use it further," Stella said eagerly.

"Ok? What are you heading?"

"I'm thinking out loud here, but if we compare an iceberg and a person..."

"If not Björn Borg, it must at least be a Swede," I said dryly, thinking about the Swedish tennis player and no 1 in the world in the late 70s; a childhood idol who basically never showed any emotions when he played.

"Ha, ha, yes probably. Anyway, Björn Borg might be a bit extreme and compared to an iceberg when he was on the tennis court, because he knew how to focus his energy. However, he too was once a newborn baby and we sometimes describe a baby as a blank sheet of paper, don't we? Open to all possibilities, sensitive, receptive and all that we are as newborns, and all that implies."

Stella was enthusiastically leading us on.

"Yes?"

"Amazing little things, full of energy and feelings and with no ego structure yet. They just make themselves heard when something needs to be taken care of. They are totally dependent on others and adjust to their surroundings to ensure that at least their basic survival needs are met. Then drop by drop, layer by layer, their ego or personality structure and maybe expectations build up." Stella paused.

"And here I have a feeling that image of the growing iceberg comes into the picture, doesn't it?" I smiled at her.

"Yep, here we can bring in the iceberg," Stella agreed.

"So, we could say that the creation of the ego is something we unconsciously learn, primarily in order to survive?" I asked.

"That's perhaps moving forward a bit fast I'd say, but partly, yes; that's what it seems like. But the creation of the ego, or the 'I', is also a basic and necessary step in our development. It's part of realising that we are not the same unit as our mother anymore. According to some, this adjusting to the environment expresses itself not only in our psyches and belief systems, but also in our bodies. Of course, our genes have a say here too, but maybe the organism's selection of what to activate when, is influenced by our environment and events in life."

Stella reached for some water.

"So, this also means that there are enough reasons not to be so hard on ourselves when we react or behave in a certain way, or can't change certain patterns, because of these old protection and survival mechanisms, doesn't it?" I observed.

"Yes." Stella nodded and continued. "It is a lot about biology, brain functioning and wiring. Nevertheless, when we realise this, we should not use it as an excuse to keep on behaving as we do when this could be viewed as unconstructive or inappropriate in today's situation. Instead, we might say, 'Hey, amazing how this helped me to survive as a child and grow up into who I am today'. However, today I'm no longer that dependent child, but an adult who can take care of my own needs and gradually become more conscious about my behaviour. Hopefully, this means that when I see fit, I can choose a way that is more appropriate for the adult, rather than run the old programme. The adult basically has his or her freedom, with all it might bring. This might be something not all of us like to see, because with freedom comes responsibility."

"Ha, yeah, we could leave that last part out, couldn't we?"

I thought of my co-worker whom I thought had not taken responsibility for his actions – or non-actions – at work.

"Well, if we do, we also deny the 'good news' in it – that we can actually do something about it, whatever the 'it' is we're dealing with; at least to some extent."

"Ooops, no more excuses then."

I was beginning to realise I probably had some action to take.

"Nope. And do you know what else just came to me?"

"Tell me."

"By excusing ourselves, we obviously don't take responsibility, at least not full responsibility, but remain in the child we once were, and make the other one bigger than we are."

It was as if she grew bigger as she said this.

"So here we are, so-called grown-up businessmen and women, doctors, lawyers, teachers, craftsmen – you name it, walking around more like children than adults, not really knowing who we are. That's what I'd call a wake-up call." I made a little whistle.

"Maybe what we see and show – the grown-up businessman part who thinks he knows himself and what he does – corresponds to the tip of the iceberg."

Stella looked around and then back at me.

"What can I say? It certainly seems like it. No wonder many of us feel tired so often."

"How do you mean?" Stella asked and I sensed her eagerness to know.

"Well, considering the 95 to 99% that we somehow still need to carry around and keep in place, that means a lot of work for the remaining 1 to 5%."

"Indeed it does, even though I assume it keeps itself in place; at least to some extent. You know, ice cools ice. Still, imagine all the energy we use up in this and all the energy we have blocked in that iceberg."

"I'm trying, I'm trying."

I sensed that something huge was making itself clear to me and I could not look the other way anymore.

"Looking at it this way, we could say that there is a double gain in growing up in the real sense and becoming more conscious," Stella noted.

"Now, it's my turn again; how do you mean?"

"Well, one gain would be that the part we carry around and try to keep in place gets smaller and lighter, and the other gain is that the energy that was blocked before becomes available to us and can flow into some more creative use."

"So what's hindering us?"

Although I knew better, I was of course hoping for an answer that would solve this issue once and for all.

"I suppose that as long as we don't realise this, we remain on the old autopilot and now that we do see it... I don't know. It will need awareness and remembering to watch ourselves and make a choice to take the action we find appropriate in the here and now, and that will probably take some effort – at least in the beginning, while the old automatic way is... automatic."

Stella turned her palms up.

"So we'd better not give in to the law of the least resistance then?"

"No, right, we'd better not. So please remind me."

"I will when I can and, please, you remind me too when you can."

"It's a deal."

"And no expectations please!" I pleaded.

"Ha, ha, right; no expectations. We had also better find some compassion for ourselves and for others, since some parts of the brain cannot accept reason and run on old instincts. Biology you know."

"Ok, it sounds like we need to head for new experiences."

I had often wondered why I react and behave the way I do, who I really am and so on and so forth. This thing that we could call the iceberg perhaps did not give any clear answers – as if there would be any – but it did give me some hints and some understanding. In a sense, we were back to where that afternoon had begun, although I do not think either of us had the feeling of walking – or talking – in a circle. It was time to call it a day and look forward to our next occasion, whilst dealing with what life generated in the meantime, moment by moment.

Chapter 6

Stella Befriends Fears that Had Her Fooled

Fighting whatever
Fooling myself into
Fearing life
Fearing death
Which come together
Inseparably
Inevitably
Surrendering
Welcoming whatever

We had agreed to meet in a new place that had recently opened. I was curious how it would look and what they would have to offer, hoping it would not be the readymade, industrial bread and pastry. My first impressions were favourable and I liked the interior décor. It was stylish and colourful without being invasive or distracting, having what I would call an earthy and embracing feeling to it. Since I was a few minutes late, I looked around for Carl. He was there already and had found a table in a quiet corner, from where he waved at me. I went to him, we hugged and I put my things on an extra armchair.

"Would you say you feel patient today?" I thought I had to give him some kind of warning.
"Why? I mean, anything particular you want me to be patient with?" Carl asked somewhat perplexed.

"Yes, me."

"Well, I don't usually feel that patience is a key ingredient when I see you, and today feels no different. What's up?"

"Oh, I feel like I'm tumbling with some old issues and would like to share some of it with you, to say some of it out loud; then maybe it becomes clearer and easier to handle – and eventually let go of."

I realised I needed to put out some of the so-called mind-fucking I had been busy with lately, before it got me all messed up and stuck in its loops.

"Sure. I'm here. What are the issues about?"

"A number of fears I have, I'd say. For some reason, they have been activated lately. I mean, fear is no news itself; on the contrary, the fears are constant companions that I have clung to and still tend to cling to. They are familiar, like guards around my comfort zone, around the known and thus safe."

"Hmm, yeah, I think I can relate to that one."

Carl seemed to be with me.

"Yes, I guess it's part of the human condition and as much as I tend to not like these fears, I also gratefully see that they have, in some sense, contributed to keeping me alive, although perhaps not always living. What might have become clearer these past few years, is some kind of realisation about how these fears have run me and how I live my life – and to some extent still do. Nevertheless, somehow existence has brought me to where I am now, to moments when energy and enthusiasm have awakened.

"Although the fears are not there in quite the same way as they used to be, I do have moments when I long for more; long to dare more, long to live more and want to love more, not just survive or feel lukewarm while waiting for whatever awaits in the end."

My mouth was too dry to continue talking and I was becoming short of breath, so I stopped and took a deep breath and some water. I surprised myself by how much I needed to get it out and not just keep it bottled up inside and keep up.

"I'm glad you said you see a difference from before, because what I heard you say and what I've seen of you don't quite match to me. It sounds like something old has got a grip again," Carl suggested.

"Yeah, you probably have a point there, but you know how it is; these old programmes do have a tendency to linger and take whatever opportunity they find to resurface, even if they are outdated."

I was often stunned by the efficiency of that old autopilot taking over in the blink of an eye.

"They do. Any particular old fear that has popped up that you would like to tell me about?" Carl looked curiously at me.

"Uhmm, this time, I think mainly the fear of not being able to break out of old patterns – and that said, the underlying fear of doing so; the feeling of being wrong, the fear of being perceived as wrong, of doing the wrong thing, of doing things incorrectly, of saying the wrong thing. Behind it, I guess, is the longing for love, a sense of belonging, the feeling of being good enough, for acceptance and approval – from others of course, but also, and maybe first and foremost, from myself.

"It is kind of funny, for all these different fears that have come up, a one-liner from Osho has come up too, since – luckily – he is also keeping me company: *'Accept yourself in tremendous gratitude. Whatsoever is, is, and it can't be otherwise.'* And it can't, since it

43

is, and is the way it is, and I do. At least sometimes."

I emptied the glass of water in front of me before I looked at Carl, while thinking that having Osho in my life was probably a life saviour in its very own way. I had since long lost count of the number of times listening to him as a way of meditating had made me relax and given me some distance to quite maddening thoughts and inner critics. I often ended up having a good laugh at myself instead, or received an energy boost that I much needed, or something else; in short he has supported my – at least – relative sanity.

"That's a good one. To me, that's a sign that the old patterns now have some competition; otherwise, my goodness, your thoughts really must be exhausting and limiting sometimes." Carl shook his head.

"Indeed; tell me about it! Fortunately, the words from Osho usually help me gain more of a perspective on things – and on me." I heard myself laugh and sigh simultaneously.

"So, what's the next one?" Carl asked.

"The next...I guess the fear of showing what I feel: vulnerability, sadness, anger, longing, love, joy...which I sensed that it wasn't allowed, 'before'. Sometimes I'm so afraid of being too needy, too much, not enough; of being rejected, not loved, not needed, not accepted, not welcome, not worthy. Even – or particularly – with those whom I would call my closest friends; friends I love deeply and I 'know' love me too, including you, since you are the ones I am really afraid of losing. That fear can then keep me from connecting with you, or from reaching out, or sharing, or asking for what I need. Instead, I often withdraw until it passes, and/or get sad, moody – or both."

"May I suggest something here?"

Carl leaned forward slightly, put his arms on the table and took one of my hands, which were already resting there, fiddling occasionally with the cup.

"Of course, please do," I answered.

"I really think you should re-phrase, change from present tense to past tense, because that would feel much more in accordance with what is the case now. At least from my point of view."

He squeezed my hand as to emphasise what he had just said.

"Yeah, maybe. Ok, I'll give it a try." I swallowed. "Past tense: It did feel safest to try to keep it inside, to hold it, to hold it in, hold it back, in control, or not even feel, so much, so often, for so long. Sometimes the inner pressure became very big, sometimes it was leaking a bit and at other times the surface cracked with more force than that. Sometimes the energy found an outlet, instead of going deadlock in one way or the other."

I internally noted that Carl was right; the past tense did make what I said feel differently, and I felt more calm and relaxed.

"Yay, that's the way! What's the Osho for this one?" Carl encouraged.

"Ehmmm...how about, *'There is no greater risk than suppression. If you suppress, you will lose all zest for life, all enthusiasm.'*"

"Can't argue with that, can I?" Carl smiled.

"No, I don't think so," I agreed, thinking about all the energy used up in suppression rather than some constructive and creative act.

"Please continue; I kind of like it."

"Like it??" I was beginning to question his taste.

"Yes, you know, like you said, when you put

things like this out, they somehow lose their grip, don't they?"

"Let's assume so."

It felt like I probably sounded more sceptical than I intended, so I continued.

"But yes, it does feel like a little more distance and less identification may happen," I admitted and carried on. "Okay, by controlling, I closed myself in, and you could say I thereby rejected myself. Not knowing how to behave, I pulled back, felt like an outsider, felt wrong; thus the autopilot brought me to exactly where he asserted we should avoid going. Fooled by my inner judge, who at the same time was on to me for trying to do as he said, for trying to please him – Joseph Heller's Catch 22, wouldn't you say?" I smiled at Carl.

"You and me and a few more of us I'd say. Could I have an Osho-quote please? That's really the best part! No offence; I like your part too," Carl reassured with a smile.

"I couldn't agree with you more. Ok, here we go: *'If you want to do something with darkness, you will have to do something with light.'*"

I switched on the torch app on my phone and directed it at him. It is true, I thought; when I find myself in darkness – inner or outer – the only way to make things easier and brighter is to bring in or get some light; light a candle, or maybe call a friend. Surely it is often easier said than done, but living has its challenges and contrast is needed, or it all becomes a blur. Maybe these days most people have a smartphone rather than a candle, and it is apparently useful for both. I could not help but smile.

"Now that's another good one and you apparently have enlightened me." Carl looked pleased. "So, we

46

really do need to pay attention to where we put our focus and energy, don't we?"

"It most likely helps, together with what we could call awareness. Well, I guess awareness is the foundation. Unless we are in actual physical danger or under threat of it, which would be when fear is actually needed as an appropriate survival mechanism, what are these fears, other than the ego's projections of the past onto the future? Projections of what no longer is, onto what is not yet; while life is what is going on here and now! It is amazing how this can be so difficult to remember." I wiggled my head like Indians often do.

"Yeah, we don't always make it easy for ourselves, do we?" Carl stated.

"No, we often don't. You know, it's almost funny, but most of us can admit to a fear of death. I mean that's more or less how we live our lives; so afraid of death that we pretend it isn't there, that it won't happen – at least not to us."

"Well, at least in Western society," Carl agreed.

"Yes, and that's where we live, isn't it? The thing is, this fear of death actually makes us afraid of life."

I could feel how I was really working myself up; my rate of speech increased, my mouth became drier, I began to perspire and I almost stumbled over the words.

"I'm afraid I don't quite follow you right now."

Luckily, Carl was a patient sounding board.

"Let's hope I follow myself. All these fears I described and which we said are largely human…"

I paused to drink some more water and dry my forehead.

"Yes?"

"They keep us from doing certain things or being a

47

certain way, because we are afraid of rejection, of not being loved, or whatever, and that would feel like dying in a way. That's how we feel, right? Yet many of us would probably like to think that we are run by what we want, but for most of us it's more likely the fear of what we don't want that runs our life."

Carl nodded slowly in agreement.

"Things and ways that probably, if we take the risk and maybe even discover that what we were afraid of didn't happen – or that the thought was worse than reality, would make us feel more alive."

I took a deliberate breath.

"Ok, now I follow. So what can we do?"

"Yeah, what can we do? I wish I had the answer to that. Feel the fear and do it anyway could be one step. One thing that I have realised for myself – and the so-called fear of death – is that perhaps it isn't so much fear of death really, but fear of the dying process, of the finishing phase of life. A fear of ending up helpless, dependent and stuck with only the staff in a hospital, or other kind of 'waiting room' – not that there is anything wrong with them."

I described a dreaded scenario.

Carl swallowed a bite of the tuna and salad wrap he had ordered. From his expression, it looked as though it might become his favourite at this place.

"Sorry, but yeah, hospital food is a horror for sure, especially compared to this and what you and I prefer to eat."

"Yes, exactly; just the thought of it makes me nauseous."

I remembered when I had had to stay in hospital.

"Anyway, I have realised that it's the fear of ending up feeling bitter and lonely, with a feeling,

48

which I wouldn't want, of not having lived as fully as I could have. If I can stop giving energy to those negative aspects and instead nourish their positive counterpoles, like joy, love and aloneness, and really live and enjoy life whatever it brings, then it shouldn't really matter where I am; in hospital or not. Friends may come if they want – or not. That said, I must confess that it would be much nicer if someone I loved would like to be there, holding me, not least when I'm counting the last breaths – and not only then, I have to add."

I did not want to sound cocky or arrogant, since my friends are one of my most precious resources, and I most certainly would not want to deliberately distance myself from them – or my need for human, friendly, loving connection and touch, however scary it might sometimes appear to me to express that need.

"If I'm one of those you love and am still around, I'll be there," Carl said softly.

"You are. Thank you."

I looked at him and our eyes met.

"And now you will have to promise the other way around too."

"I do. Of course."

"Another thing. What have you come up with in terms of the 'positive', which we could also call 'light' considering your one-liner from Osho just before?"

"Ah right, well, for me that would be to meditate, to avoid postponing things I would like to do, to reach out to friends, to find and go with my energy and find ways of expressing and enjoying it. Those seem to be the first steps. And to be aware of my thinking and judging of course."

I remembered a very sincere and wise woman I had met a couple of times saying something like, 'Don't say you know it until you live it!' and again decided to take action.

"So how do you find your energy, as you call it; any examples for inspiration?"

"That's a very good and valid question. Finding out what feels joyful, easy, in flow with me and those around could be a hint. And then do more of that."

"Easy!" Carl laughed.

"Yes, piece of cake, right?!" I laughed too. "By the way, who gave us the idea living should be easy? Then again, what makes it difficult?"

"Well, again, for many of us in the Western world, our own thoughts to begin with, which is somehow becoming more and more obvious; not least today. We not only have a tendency to let our thinking torture us, but sometimes also the thought of what we might have thought without really being aware of it," concluded Carl.

"I guess so. Since we're on the subject, our unconscious could certainly be said to take part in the complicating process."

I was coming back to how our unconscious basically runs our lives.

"How do you mean? The iceberg again?" Carl asked with a hint of doubt.

"Well, that's most likely a part of it too, don't you think? Someone whom I dare say I know cares for me, once said that in some sense I have crippled myself and that one consequence is that no one dares to come close. As we know and can see, the hands, feet, mouth, eyes; everything I need to reach out and to express myself has been affected. It also gives visible signs as to how afraid I have been – and sometimes still am – to do that."

I reached for the cup and realised that the inner activation had cooled down.

"In my world, that really is stretching it a bit far, but if you're open to hearing and absorbing something like that, then…yeah, if you say so; maybe it can change something in a helpful direction. To me that would take guts, but then again, I'd say that you do seem to have that."

We gazed into each other's eyes and sat in silence for a moment.

"Thank you." I tried to acknowledge what he had stated. "And yes, I am very grateful to that friend too, and I'd say that what he pointed out did make a difference to me – both at the time, and with time, albeit in different ways."

"Could you explain that some more, please? I'm curious. Maybe I'm a bit thick-headed, but I don't quite follow."

"You're definitely not thick to me! I'll try, since you ask me to, but I haven't really put it into words before. I'd say that the immediate effects were that I really got in touch with my vulnerability and could stay in it; not that I had much choice, really." I felt a smile growing with that memory. "Then, at least for a while, I'd say I was more…present. The senses became really important; tastes, smells, touch, textures and the beauty in different ways all around me. With time, I think I actually dared to reach out and connect much more than I used to."

I knew I would always be grateful to that friend and for that precious landmark moment. Luckily, I have experienced more of that kind of moment too, both with him and other deeply loved friends.

"And take the risk of rejection?" Carl smiled.

"Yes, it happens, even if that might really feel like dying; although if I didn't do it, that would be like continuing to kill myself slowly before being 'killed'. So, in order to choose life, yes, I do sometimes manage to convince myself to take the risk of 'death', which would happen anyway. I suppose you could say that that experience was a beautiful support for me to start allowing my longing to become greater than my fear. You know, the fear of dying in this case, is just the ego, but that's still a major player in most of us – certainly for me." I smiled back at Carl.

"Hang on…this is getting a bit complicated for me, but I think I understand what you mean. I'm sure you've heard it before; I think it was Soren Kierkegaard who said, 'To dare is to lose one's footing momentarily. Not to dare is to lose oneself.' According to me, you just illustrated it. Thank you for telling me."

"Well, thank you for asking and listening. It's been a while since I thought about it and now it was obviously time again. As Osho has said repeatedly, *'Life is not a problem to be solved, it is a mystery to be lived.'* And enjoyed."

"Well, that is indeed another good one."

Carl had been right. Sharing what was going on in me – and exposing my fears to him – had made me feel much more relaxed, and it had eased the charge, which usually accompanies an inner drama. It would not be a drama otherwise, but merely facts and interpretations. Expressing it in words created some distance, and made it possible to take it less seriously, even to laugh about it. When the drama happens, it is just another episode to watch on the internal screen, instead of on the exterior.

Thank heaven for my friends and other lifelines and saviours like Osho and meditation, I thought to myself as I was heading home for another discourse and perhaps also some Skyping with a friend.

Chapter 7

Carl Gives and Takes – or Perhaps Not

Being good
Giving a gift
To someone
At the other end
Being good
Giving the gift of receiving
To someone
At the other end
From someone
To someone
Between some ones

On my way from the car to the café, I had a quick look at my watch, already aware that I was late; not terribly late, but enough to make me feel guilty. Not only had I been over-optimistic about when I would be able to leave the office, but parking spaces proved to be almost non-existent in the close area, so I had to park relatively far from where I had planned to. I could only hope that I would learn something from it, like adding an extra half-hour or at least 15 minutes to my logistic plans.

As I entered, I noticed Stella sitting at a table in a corner, which was our favourite spot. For some reason, she seemed to prefer having her back to a wall. I made a mental note to ask her about it at some point. She was sitting there seemingly in her own world, but when I approached the table she turned her head towards me in a way that almost provoked tears in my eyes. I was surprised by my reaction.

"Hi Carl." Stella greeted me softly with a smile.

"Hi Stella." I swallowed.

"Something's happened? You look like you're about to cry."

"It's because of you."

"Me? What did I do?" Stella pointed to herself in surprise.

"You probably won't believe it, but your way of sitting there and turning your head just now seemed to touch something in me. Please don't ask me what, because I don't know."

"I take that as an invitation to ask." There was relief in her voice. "What?"

"Oh you…"

I realised I had virtually called upon her to ask, yet I did not know what to say now that she did. To gain some time, I carefully put down my briefcase on the next seat, took off my jacket, hung it on the back of the chair and sat down before I started trying to formulate a response.

"Hmm…appreciation of your beauty, the relaxed yet alert way you moved from what looked like being lost in your own world to welcoming me, and apparently you weren't lost; on the contrary."

"See? You knew. Let's not exaggerate, but thank you. I take that as a compliment." Stella smiled.

"You should. Now I would at least like to get something to drink. What would you like to have? The usual?"

"Yes please."

"Ok. I'll be right back."

I was happy to go and order, since I felt as though I needed a little break to collect myself again, or rather, to sense what I had just experienced and described. Back at the table, Stella's cappuccino and my double espresso filled the air with a rich note of fresh hot coffee.

"Mmmm…thank you, Carl. I love this smell. And look at that beautiful heart!"

Stella was obviously pleased. The barista performed his job to perfection and it was hopefully as much a pleasure to him as it was to us. The foam of the steamed milk looked rich and creamy and beautifully decorated with the last drops of coffee.

"Yes, good coffee is a real treat. By the way, speaking about treats, I'd like to thank you. This is all quite new to me and I really appreciate it. I mean, discovering meditation, these little come-togethers, our talks or colloquies about various issues, no pretence, no expectations; just giving each other time, attention and whatever we have to ventilate and share. It's really nurturing. Hearing myself saying this, I realise something must have happened to me, because I can hardly believe my ears, yet it is how I feel. Even that, me saying 'I feel', is really something."

"Thank you. You know, Carl, it goes both ways. Isn't that wisely arranged?"

Stella smiled and looked at me mischievously.

"I forgot to mention your sense of humour – and yes, it is, and all the better in that case."

"I think so too. And I really like 'come-togethers'," Stella said appreciatively.

"You do? I refuse to call it 'meetings', because that sounds so formal and business-like and it's not like we're dating. Come to think of it, I like it better than get-togethers. We come together for come-togethers."

"That's what we do," Stella agreed.

"What surprises me in a way, is that it feels so incredibly good and intimate and, at the same time, so effortless; apart from finding a parking spot and arriving on time, that is! Having said that, even that usually works out quite easily."

"See? Something or someone seems to want us do this."

"Luckily and to my pleasure. It's like this is an opportunity to stop and to breathe, no matter what chaos is ruling at home or at work." *Or in me for that matter*, I thought to myself.

"So, how's your chaos?" Stella's down-to-earth-ness led us on.

"Do you really want to go there?"

"I asked, didn't I? I do. The question is, do *you* want to go there?"

"Yes and no, so yes. Without getting into too much detail, work chaos is falling into a little bit more of structure, so that is good, even though our last takeover project has requested more time and money than expected. Still, we finally seem to be moving ahead according to the original master plan, which is a must."

"Not that I fully grasp what you're doing, but it sounds good. And home chaos?" Stella enquired.

"Whatever I say or do seems to be wrong and whatever she says or does is wrong; then the kids on top of that. You're lucky you know."

I looked at her and had some water.

"Maybe, maybe not."

Stella made the gesture of opening her palms to something bigger and shrugged her shoulders.

"Expectation and frustration; I do usually enjoy my life and situation, but we never get to know the alternative outcomes, do we?" Stella asked rhetorically and continued, "Do you ever remind yourselves why you chose each other? And why you chose to have children?"

"Why? How do you mean?"

"Well, you both did what you did for some reasons that made the pros outweigh the cons." Stella was to the point.

"That's almost flattering. I wouldn't say it was all that consciously thought through and assessed, you know."

I felt my cheeks burning, which she noticed.

"Hot subject, huh? To be honest, I didn't think so either, but still, it might be worthwhile to give it some consideration, even for the two of you. Of course, it doesn't have to happen now."

"You mean, what attracted us to each other, what kept us together, what keeps us together, why we wanted to have children?"

I thought I could see what Stella was aiming at.

"Something like that. And perhaps also what you expect from each other, what you would like to have, what you think and feel you get and don't get."

"Wow! Did you ever consider counselling?" I laughed.

"Sorry, I didn't mean to pretend to know better or meddle into your personal business." Now it was Stella's turn to blush.

"Ha, ha, there's nothing like natural make-up, right? Come on, seriously, what else do we do here besides meddling in each other's business and solving the world's problems on the way?"

"You're right; and hopefully meddling in our own business too," Stella admitted.

"Yes, that too. To me, you most certainly have more than one point here. I mean, I guess both Donna and I feel like we give more than we get; then we get frustrated, moody and bitchy and even mean sometimes. I often prefer to work late, rather than go home in time for dinner, or to play with Eric and Flore. If I do, I'm often far too busy with the phone or computer anyway. Shit! They really don't deserve that."

I could see a pattern with which I was not overly contented.

"No, they don't. And what you said about giving; did you actually hear that?" Stella was back to her alert self again.

"What?" The kids had remained in my mind.

"That you feel like you give more than you get in return."

"Yes… and?" I was confused.

"Maybe this appears blunt to you, but one could say that sounds more like a business deal than a love relationship. It's as though you think you don't get enough value for what you're paying or putting in."

"Come on Stella!" I obviously felt a bit hurt.

"No, honestly. Have a look at it. If you truly give something, you don't expect anything in return, do you? If giving is not unconditional, it isn't really giving; then it is some kind of business, overt or covert, conscious or unconscious. Come to think of it, that's even stated in the legal definition of a gift, if I remember my law classes correctly."

Stella was as firm and relentless as she could be sometimes and I somewhat vainly wished for an escape.

"And how often do you think what we call giving is really unconditional?" I asked, almost grumpily.

Apparently, she had hit a sore spot.

"Well, that's a different story and maybe in Utopia, but let's keep that for later, shall we?"

I almost reluctantly nodded in agreement and Stella continued.

"In relationships, there is also the question of balance; of giving and receiving, of giving back a little more of the good stuff and a little less of the so-called bad stuff. That way the relationship has the potential to grow into something you will enjoy and like to stay in. At least that is a conclusion the psychotherapist Bert Hellinger made. It does make sense to me."

"That's certainly a new way of looking at it, at least in my world – and Donna's, I dare say. I must admit, it's worth looking at like you said. I just wish I were able to convey it in a way so that Donna and I could talk about it too without arguing for once. We seem to have this talent to make each other angry these days."

"Well, that's a good sign in a way, isn't it?"

"It is? Would that by any chance go for disappointment as well?"

"Why?" Stella asked.

"It's just that I've repeatedly been told that I disappoint her and the children by doing or not doing this or that," I sighed.

"Hmm, I'd say it does," Stella confirmed.

"Really? How?" Her answer took me by surprise.

"If you have a careful look at it, maybe you would agree that it is *because* you love each other that you get angry, and *because* you love someone, they can disappoint you. Someone you don't really care about doesn't really bother you either, does she? That just wouldn't be someone you would waste that time and energy on."

"Well, except for the stranger who runs into me in the street." I could think of more than one incident like that.

"Now, what if he's just an excuse or trigger for anger which is already there? If you didn't walk around with suppressed anger inside, you could probably just smile at him and say something like, 'Hey, your legs seem to work faster than your eyes!' or similar." Stella smiled.

"Ha, ha, that's a thought, but looking at it like that, both the anger and the disappointment could be good signs, you mean? I think I get your point, and actually that also gives us a kind of foundation to work from. Again, I just have to find a way to get that through to her." I could hear the tiredness in my voice.

"We all have our challenges, don't we?" Stella encouraged. "But if she's half as motivated as you seem to be right now, behind that lurking resignation, I for one have good hope."

"Let's hope you're right, but if she isn't, she isn't. We soon will find out." The one conclusion I could make.

"You will. In connection with that, another thing just came to mind. In general terms, have you ever tried to give or offer something that wasn't really received?" Stella inquired.

"Hmm…yes, I have."

61

"And how did that make you feel?"

"Well, sometimes rather hurt, or worthless and stupid, I guess." I was beginning to wonder where this was heading.

"So looking at it more closely, one could perhaps say that not receiving a gift – or an offer – is like a kind of rejection?"

"Yes, you actually could say that." I looked at her perplexed.

"The next step then could be that the giver should be grateful if the gift is received, right?"

"Yes, Stella; point made, point taken. One other aspect of this I'd say would be that sooner or later at least, we stop trying to give where we don't feel received, and move on."

I looked at Stella who nodded in agreement.

"One thing I wonder though…"

"What?"

"When do love relationships turn into these business-like dealings?"

"You tell me. Maybe I'm sticking my neck out here, but looking around I'd almost say that marriage seems to be a contributing factor."

Stella gave me an almost mischievous look.

"Hear! Hear! Please elaborate; this could be interesting."

I looked down at my ring and turned it a little.

"I thought all women, including you, wanted to get married?" I said teasingly.

"Yeah, I'm every woman. No, big mistake; your mistake." Stella countered.

"Well, I do remember you wanting to get married." I had to insist on this one.

"That was before I started looking beyond the wedding day and realised what that marriage contract actually seems to bring with it in so many cases. Well, the wedding day, too, in terms of expectations and frustration and not least the amount of money usually spent. Like a friend of mine said, 'I'd rather build a new terrace!'" Stella asserted.

"Aha, marriage contract, business deal, but your friend isn't very romantic, is she? Or maybe it's a he?"

"Ha, ha, who knows, but yes, we're getting there, aren't we? You sign the papers and something in you relaxes – and not necessarily in a beneficial way. Done deal. Hopefully, the honeymoon phase will last for a while, but then eventually everyday life takes over; children, activities, logistics. It's like an enormous jigsaw puzzle. It amazes me how you and Donna and so many others basically manage to put the pieces in place and stay together. Seeing and hearing about this daily challenge often makes me feel even more happy and relieved about the way my life has turned out so far." She smiled.

"That sounds familiar. The everyday puzzle, I mean." I nodded and shook my head almost simultaneously.

"And more often than not, the priority is no longer with the couple's relationship, so the spice, caring and attraction have a tendency to fade out, at least for many," Stella argued.

"We no longer feel the need or desire to make a little effort for the other person – and ourselves, like we did when dating or during the honeymoon. Since the marriage vows or 'contract' are there, we unconsciously believe that effort is not required." I understood exactly what she meant.

"A normal process, I guess," she continued, "but when you start taking your partner for granted and don't really bother, then other things and others can suddenly make you – or your partner – more eager."

"I'd say this even happens with couples who aren't married, but ok, I see your point. I get the impression that some marriages seem to keep more of the original flavour?" I did not want to give up so easily.

"I agree, and those I know who keep nourishing their relationship by making time for each other and, paradoxically, giving each other time and space of their own, have easier lives. I can't remember where it came from, but I once heard or read that love in togetherness is a flow, and love in aloneness is silence. It stayed with me and I find it beautiful."

I could tell that she really did and the fragrance of it was lingering with her. Stella looked at me. My interest must have shone through, so she continued.

"Besides the beauty, there is a truth – or whatever you would call it – in that, and I am happy to say that I feel I have experienced – and experience – both; at times anyway." She smiled at me.

"Would you tell me some more, please?"

This was a subject most certainly worth exploring further. Hopefully it was to Stella too.

"Well, you probably agree with me that love, silence and flow are somehow beyond words and cannot be ordered, but let's see what comes. Love in togetherness; what comes to mind first for most of us, I think, is a couple-relationship. I have a feeling you too have experienced moments or times with a partner, when there has been this effortless inner and outer movement of coming close together, and then giving each other space and being apart for a while; like waves, or flow. To me, it's when love and acceptance rule rather than expectations, ideas, envy, jealousy and possessiveness –you name it. It's also when you have this feeling of understanding and being a 'team' without having to say or explain too much; when you instinctively know where you have each other."

"I have." I smiled at her.

"I thought so. Actually, I know you have. We have." She smiled back at me.

"And we do. I mean, having spent much of my adulthood so far without a significant other, but with a number of others who are significant to me, I would also include friendship in the togetherness, and I feel it holds as true there too. About love in aloneness – well, when I accept myself as I am, with no judgements on how I look, on what the body does or doesn't do, on what I think, feel and say, or do or don't; when I'm just being here the way I am, there is also a deep silence inside. It's a silence that probably also pervades into the outer somehow."

The words naturally faded away and silence enveloped us for a while, despite the external noise.

"Mmmm, yeah...silence...flow. Like I said, it looks like Donna and I have some challenges ahead and, after this, I actually feel quite eager to go ahead."

"Life would probably turn out quite boring without them," Stella consoled.

"Ha, ha, yes probably, and like you say, married or not, we all get our different lots, don't we?"

"That seems to be the way it is, primrose path or not," Stella concluded.

My eagerness had become stimulated during our talk and all of a sudden I could not wait to get home to

Donna and the children. Stella's pointing out to me some new perspectives on giving, and perhaps not so much taking as receiving and flowing, felt like a gift and tool that I would like to use in our family. I figured the best way to make that happen would be to act accordingly, rather than tell them; that is, to walk the talk without the talk, at least to begin with, which would be a healthy challenge to myself. Who knows, maybe we could even make it a primrose path; at least certain parts of it.

What also stayed with me was how I had seen myself as not really being there emotionally when I was there physically, like with the children for instance. We may not have realised it at the time, but what I liked about 'before' (before the smartphone era), is that there seemed to be time for everything in its time and a satisfaction in doing one thing at a time, instead of now when basically everything can be done at any time. This often seems to bring a kind of fake sense of efficiency; we are constantly multi-tasking with the resulting frustration of never getting anything done properly – like being fully there playing with the kids, or watching a movie without sending a text or checking my emails. I would also give myself the challenge of putting the phone away with flight mode on upon entering the house, and as much as possible stick to office work at the office and family time at home. And so be it.

Chapter 8

Stella Feels Incompatible with Herself

How are you doing?
Fine, thank you
Even though I'm dying
And so too are you
We just don't know when
So instead of just enduring
Better off enjoying now, then

"I must say that I think you're dealing with it astonishingly well."

Carl's statement puzzled me a little, since I felt it came out of the blue and I had no idea to what he was referring.

"Dealing with what?" I had to ask.

"The diseases, the body, all the challenges you have to face."

"Well, thank you, I guess. But just so you know, I do have my moments."

I still did not quite get what this was all about.

"Of course. I kind of hope you do, and that's part of it too," Carl maintained.

"What do you mean?"

"You're an alive human being for God's sake, not a robot. If you didn't have your moments, that would be scary, I'd say."

"If I were a robot, I wouldn't have become sick." I smiled.

"Don't fool yourself; robots break and get viruses and all kinds of system failures too."

"Yeah, right; they do." I couldn't help but laugh.

"So, would you please give me one?" Carl insisted.

"Give you one what?"

I really started to feel as though we were not only from, but also on different planets.

"An example of one of those moments."

"Are you kidding me?"

I was perhaps dodging a bit, since I was not so sure I wanted us to discuss this subject.

"No, I'm not. I would like you to tell me, since I have not yet experienced one with you," Carl persuaded.

"Well, be careful what you wish for. You could say that I have been trying to keep them to myself as much as possible."

"I bet there are many of us who would like to be there for you and with you, should you want or need us to."

"You do? That's kind. Thank you." I was touched.

I looked down at the table and took a deep breath before I looked at Carl and continued.

"You know, I'm really grateful that I do have experienced that already, so I will try to remind myself next time."

More than once I had been described as 'independent' and that would be one side of the coin. I had come to realise that independence is frequently spiced with stubbornness and pride, which conceal and maybe compensate for the fear of being, doing, or saying something wrong. It's the fear of rejection, of needing help and support, of being perceived as too needy, of being a burden, of being vulnerable and dependent and of no one being there when the need or surrender happens. And friends have been there, even though, on some level, I have often done my best to do what I fear the most – to scare them away.

"Please do." Carl was really patient.

"So what is it you want to know?"

I hoped that maybe I could keep it brief and specific.

"What you think, what you feel, what you do in those moments?"

"Mamma mia…ermmm…I guess sometimes it just gets a bit much, almost overwhelming, and I simply want to get away and out of it. Especially when something 'new' happens, adds on, before I have adjusted to it. Sometimes when I fall, or drop something a little too often, or when cramps or aches are there a little too much, or my eyes are so dry that it hurts to keep them open, or I can't really see…then I sometimes get so bloody mad – and sad, too. Why me? Why all this shit? It's too much, too early; it's not fair. All the things that somehow work against each other, in me, against me. It sometimes feels like I'm not compatible with myself in so many ways."

"How do you mean? I understand that a lot of it is autoimmune, but…"

"Yeah, that's what I could call the medical, allopathic, or biological foundation, which the doctors use." I paused. "For instance, the way my hands and fingers have become; I cannot give myself the eye drops that I need a lot of. My feet, legs and poorly functioning lungs make it difficult to exercise or even to walk and maintain my balance. Even if I have time to take a walk at my pace, I still cannot be too far from home or a toilet because…well, what the heck, I might

69

as well bring it all into the open; the muscles don't hold it together so well."

I looked at Carl to see if I had gone too far; since he had asked, I just wanted to be frank about the situation, not provocative. He looked concerned and remained silent. I saw the amusing side of what I had just admitted. Often, I could not help but laugh about these different things happening to me; otherwise I would probably be in serious trouble.

"It is kind of symbolic isn't it? Regardless of how desperately I try, the body knows better and doesn't always hold it together so well. Anyway, at times it feels like it adds up, and this is just part of the list. Oh, I should stop right there; you don't want to hear or know all this."

I stopped, felt a little shaky, and hoped he would not think I was pitying myself, or seeking pity. I would not want that.

"What you just described would be more than enough for anyone. And I do want to know, as long as it is alright for you to talk about it, otherwise I wouldn't have asked in the first place."

The sincere tone of Carl's voice and the concern in his eyes moved me.

"Yeah, maybe. So, like I said, there are moments when I feel it's unfair, too much, and I'm afraid of what might come and how soon. I'm afraid I will end up without someone to be there for me, with me. At the same time, how could I expect anyone to be there? Everybody is busy with their own life, and rightly so. So, there is fear of becoming dependent, helpless and a burden, but also a fear of being 'abandoned' and lonely."

I realised I had accelerated my speech and detached from really feeling what I had just said. Strangely enough, at the same time, I felt relieved to get it out in the open.

"And of pain? I mean physical pain?" Carl asked.

"I was almost about to say no, but yes, of course, if I could choose, I would not like to have pain – like I had when it all started and like it has been since, in the more active periods or relapses."

I was actually happy to be reminded; that made the present situation even more enjoyable. Almost saying "no" was just a sign that I had been lucky enough to be in less pain for a while. In good phases like this, I sometimes take the status quo for granted and forget how incapacitating and demoralising pain can be.

"How was that?"

"Basically everything hurt; every little movement. I could hardly bear a duvet covering me, or press a handle, or turn a key in a lock, or put clothes on."

"Wow, I didn't know that." Carl made a little whistle.

"Nothing much to talk about, really, is it? But I most certainly am grateful it is not like that all the time anymore."

I smiled, partly to ease the heaviness, which I felt was lurking and partly because it was true; gratefulness was there.

"I can only imagine," Carl said slowly.

"There are other aspects too, you know…"

"Like?"

"Sorry; forget I said that. I never should have mentioned it."

I could feel some shame building up, but maybe it would be a good thing to go through that one too.

"Well, you did, so?" Carl encouraged and smiled.

"It seems so superficial, and I suppose it is, but that's part of life too. Ok, to start with I just want to make it clear that I know I could be so much worse off, and I really do appreciate everything that is still working as well as it does, and all that I still can do. At least sometimes I find my reflection in the mirror ok, but the thing is, in those other moments, all these things happening with my body have affected my appearance, as well as whatever little I had of self-esteem and self-confidence. I never really felt good about myself, or how I looked, nor believed I could be considered attractive. My body's premature decline has not made it any easier; a 'limping freak' or something like that is what a voice inside sometimes call me. Accepting, including and adjusting to the limitations to what I can do is not always without inner resistance, to put it mildly." I symbolically bit a finger.

"I imagine that telling you that you look lovely and cope wonderfully won't help, will it?

"Yes and no. I'm afraid it won't really, but nevertheless, thank you. I do need to hear it, to hear another voice besides my inner critic. I really appreciate it, even if I have difficulty believing it and taking it in," I confessed.

"Yeah? Well I wish you could. Take it in I mean, that you could just receive it."

Carl looked at me, but I found it difficult to let our eyes meet and so I shrugged my shoulders before I continued.

"Thank you... really." I looked at him gratefully and continued. "Also, with regard to all these outer feminine, or so-called sexy attributes, like certain clothes, shoes, jewellery, hairstyles and make-up etc., the range of what I can do, wear and use is so limited. It's usually much more 'basic' and focused on what does function rather than what is sexy, beautiful, or even just nice sometimes. Ok, how did we end up here? Enough of complaining and self-pity."

I thought I must have crossed a line, which it would have been better not to do if I wanted to maintain at least some of my integrity, dignity and ideas intact. I took note of my thoughts and could not help but smile internally at my vanity – and fear of losing a very dear friend.

"Ok, for the record, I asked, and to me right now anyway, it's neither about self-pity or complaining. I'm slowly beginning to get it, but you really are shit hard on yourself. You're dealing with a pretty intense and challenging situation and to me you're dealing with it in a way that I, for one, could just pray for. You have every reason to take that as a boost to your self-esteem and self-confidence, instead of the opposite. I'm not walking in your shoes, but from my perspective...shit, I wish you could really see it for yourself!"

Carl's little reprimand felt liberating and embarrassing at the same time. I realised I felt quite vulnerable.

"I don't know what to say. Could I ask you to just hold me please?"

"I was hoping you'd ask, or I would have suggested. Luckily there are some things in life for which there will never be an app."

Carl smiled, stood up, went around the table, asked me to get up and took me in his arms.

For once we had chosen a table by a sofa, which we had to ourselves, so after a long, warm hug, Carl sat down and asked if I wanted to lean against him, in his arms. I did. My eyes were burning. All of this in a public place.

"It might be frosting on the cake, you know, but I sometimes do long for someone with whom there is love and trust, to hug and lie close to. I do need someone who holds me when I am not able to hold myself, someone who holds me lovingly, firm and close, so the shell may crack and the armour fall, yet still I might allow myself to be held and cared for; to relax and rest together with someone, and feel that I not always have to hold it together and cope on my own. And also to be that someone to someone."

My voice was thick, much more than I, or rather, my pride would have wished for.

"Understandable my dear friend, and right now there is someone. I am here with you." He paused briefly and squeezed me before he continued. "Since we're anyway on the subject, and if you don't mind, how has it been for you, really, these years with the diseases and the medications? As I remember, you were pretty much avoiding painkillers even when you had severe headaches or stomach cramps."

Carl obviously would not settle with less than the whole story this time.

"Well, what can I say? I still try to avoid what I don't 'have to' take. So far, I'd say the chemo infusions have been the worst."

"You had to have chemo??" Carl asked with concern.

"Yes, different kinds at different times. My resistance was already strong when I started taking the tablets. Since then, the tablets have become something I got used to taking; almost routine. Then 'the real thing' was, how should I put it…strongly recommended. I would, of course, have preferred not to do it, but the risks were presented as high to say the least, so I really had no choice but to go through with it. 'Is this really necessary?' was my first reaction when they told me, and the answer from the doctor was: 'It's all about saving your lungs.' I thought, 'Why? Why now, after all that I have done over the last few years?' Then some kind of acceptance came to me. 'Ok, this is the way it is. This is apparently something I am supposed to do. Drop the fight. Just do it.'"

"I don't know what to say. Was it bad? Oh, I'm such a jerk – stupid question; of course it must have been."

"You're not a jerk. Well, yes, in a way my body did react very strongly, with what could easily be interpreted as a big 'No!' In a way, the strong physical reaction in the loneliness that I had feared, but it was also ok. At the same time, I was happy to be alone. I felt that I could really be with it, and be with me. There was really nowhere to go and nothing to do, except simply breathe, one breath at a time. It was like my chemo meditation. And I was lucky; I didn't lose my hair."

"That's one way of looking at it," Carl grinned.

"Yes, it is. It really was quite powerful and I was actually surprised that I could be so present and accepting of the whole situation. There was also the fear that the treatment might not work and of the long-term side-effects."

"Did it? Did it work?"

"I don't know. I mean, obviously I didn't get well, but maybe I would have been worse off than I am now without it; who knows? We'll never know the alternative consequences. I still have my original lungs, for instance. Regarding the side-effects, I don't know there either. Some I got and some are kind of irrelevant, like not being able to get pregnant, for example, and some might still pop up."

"In a way so far, so good, then?"

"Yes. By the way, or did I already tell you? 'Have trust' has come to me very strongly several times in meditation, and it no longer feels just like a challenge, but also like a reassurance. My joy and gratitude for life, my body, the relative health that made it possible to leave the hospital and being able to slowly walk back home after a couple of days, were so big. They somehow overpowered the moments of loneliness and 'abandonment' I might have feared. I've also seen that if I felt abandoned, it was primarily I who abandoned myself, by not asking someone I would have liked to be there with me to be there with me, if that was what I really wanted. As I mentioned before, I was also happily alone in that state."

I also thought about the gratitude I felt for living in a country where examinations, treatments and medications are primarily covered by the tax system. An already tough situation does not have to become a financial impossibility. It may be costly in different ways and sometimes feel almost unbearable anyway.

"Did you hear what you just said?" Carl pointed out, interrupting my thoughts.

"What do you mean?"

I positioned my head so that I could see Carl's face clearly.

"You just gave yourself the answer to what we talked about before; about fears of life and death and the last days, or weeks, or months."

"Yeah…right. Thank you for reminding me."

"Thank you for sharing this with me. I bet you haven't talked about it all that much with all that many, have you?" Carl was right.

"Well, like I said, no, I guess I haven't. And I appreciate your asking. Would you even have space for some more?"

"Absolutely."

Carl's willingness to be there for me seemed endless.

"I remember thinking that my lung condition was trying to tell me something, but I did not seem to want to listen, or to accept the message, so on some level I seemed to choose not to understand. Since I did not pay much attention, my body rang the alarm repeatedly and tried to force me, so for a while I did pay attention, and some kind of change seemed a must. Then I fell back into some kind of complacency. I also remember a dream in which the chemo didn't work, that I would need a lung transplant in just a few years, and that was scary."

"I'm surprised you called it a dream and not a nightmare," Carl remarked dryly.

"Well, I was shit scared; scared that my fears would be greater than my longings, and I would end up feeling that I had not lived or loved enough while I had the chance. Here we go again; it seems like a theme for me, doesn't it? And there was also the 'message' that 'there's nothing to do or change, just accept whatever is'. That fighting, that not letting go, sometimes became so strong, and still does. It seems to be one of these old habits I have and obviously difficult to quit. I suppose we all do what we do, until we don't."

The memory of that dream also brought up the issue of an eventual lung transplant, something I wasn't sure how I would handle, should I have to face it. Having given it some thought, I felt biased towards a 'thank you, but no thank you; the ones I have are the ones that were given to me and if they stop functioning, I stop.' As we do seem to have some kind of cellular memory, and the lungs belong to a group of very vital, essential, 'personal' organs, to just take on someone else's would presumably feel very strange to the body, and to 'me'. Still, maybe I would happily go through whatever to get to stay in this body a while longer? Or maybe not; who knows? I just knew that I did not know and, hopefully, would never find out.

To me this is one of these areas where we, with modern science, tend to make ourselves larger than life, good or bad, or maybe neither, depending on how we look at it, if we look at it. My thoughts wandered before Carl called me back. Indeed, life very often does not turn out the way we think, so I might as well not think so much.

"Or well learned. But no wonder, I'd say, and fully understandable. Maybe what I might call the fighting spirit has also been a vital part and strength during all this time, to cope the way you did? Perhaps it still is, when needed? Like they say, there's a front and a backside to everything. It seems to me as though you're much more at terms with yourself now compared to what you've described before, both in terms of fears and longings, and fighting and accepting," Carl suggested.

"Hopefully you're right. No, honestly, I agree; it usually feels that way. And you know, basically life is just too beautiful not to enjoy while it lasts and while I can. Listening to music that can take me anywhere and everywhere, seeing the rising and setting sun, enjoying the shade, the endless sky, the moon, the stars, the woods and the trees mirrored in a lake, the play of the clouds, the colours, hearing the birds sing, feeling the soft, moist grass under my feet, smelling flowers, tasting ripe raspberries and strawberries, hanging out and sometimes cuddling with friends like right now, you name it; love is in the air just like that. Life and existence are miracles and I'm here, we're here, now, a part of it. Wow!"

"Yes, we are! Wow!"

Having a number of diagnoses like lupus, scleroderma, neuropathies and a few more in the bag, my main strategy had been not to give it too much attention; at least not more than necessary. I was not one of those people who spent hours on the Internet looking for information to prepare myself for what may come one day, or to prepare for the doctors' appointments. I had had the intention of not letting it interfere with my life; I wanted to go on as if nothing had happened. Only, in the long run, that did not work. It was as if I did not want my body – with all the symptoms it carried – to be a part of me, of my life. I didn't realise that the body in fact is my life, my home in this life, the physical foundation for it, even though I have also discovered that there is more to it than that; that I am more than the body, not less.

Sharing with Carl was also like sharing with myself. Being there for me with so much loving care and attention, was as if he held a mirror in which I

79

could see things and myself more clearly, and allow myself to be seen and heard both by him and me. Luckily, my friends are generally better friends to me than I am – or rather than some of the voices inside of me are...or were. It sometimes seems like such a loud crowd inside and that the one person missing is me, my voice. Perhaps a step forward would be to pay less attention to those other voices and instead see what or who is really there.

One day, shortly after that talk, when I was cleaning and organising my desk drawers, I found, by coincidence, a poem among the notes and papers, describing how I had felt at one point.

At times
I look into a mirror
And see a freak
At times
I look into a mirror
And see a sweet woman
At times
The cons
Feel many, too many
At times
Counting
Is not an issue
At times
Being with what is
Is what is

Being in a body with a number of challenges is also a gift. The reminders I get to stay in the present, that life and the body with all its incredible functions are not to be taken for granted and that life itself is a gift, not a right, are precious. Yet, to be honest, sometimes I miss what has been lost; sometimes I envy people who can do things I would like to do and cannot, or else am not willing to pay the price for, or make the effort. For instance, there are blind people who go skiing and other heroes like that, but I am not one of them. So, moments like that are there too. Allowing these thoughts to drift through my mind and being aware of what I focus on is, however, a good one, as is to make do with and the best out of what is, and what I have. Living it all, as long as it lasts, is enough, is already a lot.

Chapter 9

Carl Considers Concepts of Reality - or Maybe Relativity

It seems like a lifetime ago
And was just yesterday
It seems like yesterday
And was a lifetime ago
Time so illusory
Is what we make of it
Tomorrow today will be yesterday
And tomorrow never comes
Since now always is

It was time again to meet with Stella. It felt like it had been a while since we last saw each other, perhaps a couple more weeks than usual, but paradoxically it also felt like time had passed quickly. Like always, I had been quite busy at work and at home with the family. When I entered the café and saw her, I became a little concerned. We hugged, fetched our coffees, and settled down.

"You look a bit…kind of…sad today. What's up?"
I hadn't seen Stella looking this low since we started seeing each other again.
"I do? Well, I can't really hide the way I feel right now, even if I wanted to. I don't think I have ever been known to have a poker face." Stella forced a smile.
"Oh, I'm not so sure about that. What happened?"

"I don't know really...life I guess." Stella answered a little evasively.

"And what does that mean?"

"I'm not really sure why or when it started, but I seem to be having one of these dips into a black hole. It's as if the part of me that feels so incredibly lost, worthless and lonely takes over and runs the show for a while. When it happens, I'm usually awful around people, so I actually thought about cancelling today. Instead, I decided to take a step out of the usual pattern of withdrawal and isolation and come anyway. But I'd better warn you, and ask you to stop me please if I become too critical, cynical and horrible to be around."

"I can't really see that happening, but if it does I will let you know. And I'm glad you came." I did my best to reassure her.

"Thank you. Let's hope you still feel that way when we leave." There was a hint of that cynicism she had mentioned.

"Ha, ha, yeah, let's hope. So you have no clue what triggered it?"

"Well, I guess there are several aspects working together; it's like an inner pinball game with the ball flipping around."

"Aha?"

I thought about bringing in some humour, but it felt inappropriate. I reminded myself to just shut up and listen, even though I imagined it would not last very long, no matter how good my intention was.

"Do you remember I told you about how much I looked forward to spending a couple of weeks with some very dear friends of mine?" Stella asked.

"Yes I do. Didn't it work out like you had hoped?"

"On the contrary; it was wonderful," Stella enthused.

"I'm getting confused here."

"Hang in there please. Like I said, I had a wonderful time with lots of laughter, closeness and talking. I suppose that what you could call the little child inside of me wished it could last longer, wished for more of it and felt sad when it was time to say goodbye. The more reasonable grown up in me who was grateful for those weeks was dominated by the little one sulking about past unfulfilled needs and emotions."

Stella looked almost embarrassed by her admission and I could actually see the little girl in her.

"Sorry, but please let us come back to the little one and big one later. For now, please continue."

Stella had aroused my interest and I wanted to talk more about it at some point, although we had touched on it before.

"Ok, remind me please when you're up for it. So, I guess it was a bit too much for 'the little one' to say goodbye to some of the people she loves the most. Another aspect is that it is a bit like when you've been in a light and cosy room and then go out into the cold and dark, or even just look out at it. Then it's really dark and difficult to see anything, until your eyes adjust and you realise you can actually see and discern things more easily. Last week, I was also reminded of a few things about myself that felt pretty painful and frustrating."

"Ouch! Would you like to tell me about them...or not? Feel free."

I did not want to put any pressure on her, knowing from my own experience that when that happens to me I often shut down.

"Well, one thing is the feeling deep down in me that I don't really belong, which seems to have compelled me to try and justify being 'here', my existence, by being good and nice, by figuring out others' needs before they ask, by not creating trouble, or being too much or not enough. You know; we've been there before. Then it all starts twisting and turning. What went wrong? What should I do in this life? Why do I still put others' needs before my own? Do I even know what my needs are? When the shit hits the fan, even: Why don't I have, or rarely even get into an intimate relationship? On top of that are some bodily reminders."

"Well, those thoughts could all drive me kind of crazy too. I get a little bit upset, though."

"Why?" Stella looked confused.

"I neither can, nor want, to take away your feelings, but to me nothing went wrong, except maybe the part where you got sick, which I could say feels somehow unfair to me, but I see a lovely woman in front of me who deserves it all as much as anyone."

"So what went wrong?"

Stella blushed and smiled, despite – or maybe because of – the question and my feedback.

"Come on, stop it! Nothing went wrong; you're just dipping like you said. And what did you mean by being impossible around people?"

"This." Her eyes avoided mine and looked around and at the ceiling, then hesitantly looked at me again. "Like I said, critical, cynical, moody, bitchy, cut off, 'mind-y', dismissive. It's like all defences get activated when I'm in this very small and vulnerable place, and I may even lash out and attack – verbally that is – in order to keep people at bay, unconsciously of course, until I see it; and sometimes I can't help myself even when I do see it. All thorns out. Maybe you could say I go limbic. The paradox is that what I really need, want and long for, in spite of thorns out and guns on my hips, is for someone I love to see me, to see the pain and fears behind the whole cover-up, and just tell me that I'm ok, that it's going to be ok; to somehow hold me and hold the space for me, and just let me be small and vulnerable, but not alone and lonely in this – like you just did and do. And I 'know' that first and foremost I am the one who has to do it for me; that I can't put that on someone else. The bottom line is that when I fall into this state, it feels like I was given a deck of cards, only there are no instructions and I'm not smart enough to figure out how to play them."

"May I say that you are very ok and I appreciate you telling me all this. I may not have told you for a long time, but I really love you, even more today than yesterday and probably less than tomorrow."

I did not want to comfort her; it was more like stating things as they were to me.

"How come you've become so sweet? Or is my memory failing me?" She smiled coyly, as did I.

"It must be your influence, so let's leave memory out of the game for now."

"Ok, as you wish. Speaking of yesterday, today, tomorrow, you, me and others, I guess comparison does play a part too."

"Comparison with whom, with what?" I wondered.

"No one or nothing in particular; more in general. Expectations, for example, and with them frustration.

Did you ever hear that one before?" Stella raised her eyebrows and continued. "Comparison really is making a bed for misery; I mean, you can always find someone or something that you don't measure up to, and boom, falling is a 'fact'." She looked a little discontented.

"So, you mean comparing yourself to people with, say, a healthy, functioning body, in a so-called intimate relationship, having sex maybe every other Saturday with one or two kids fighting about the remote or iPad outside the bedroom, toys to stumble over all over the place, an allegedly busy, more important career than your partner's, with competitive colleagues and a controlling boss, a lawn that needs mowing or else the neighbours will start complaining, makes you feel like shit?" I described life in the suburbs and we both laughed.

"Exactly," she teased back.

"Yeah, you go on with that then." I shook my head.

It is funny how easy it is to imagine life as in the fairy tales; then we find ourselves watching so-called reality shows on TV.

"Ha, ha, I most likely will, since I do keep falling, which also means that I keep on rising to something else in between," Stella reflected.

"Right! And come to think of it, you ought to fall literally and, like you say, fortunately, you do rise again – more often than most of us, speaking of comparisons."

"You mean because of my…hmmm…bodily flaws."

"Now we're talking."

"Well, I don't know if this is of any comfort to you, but I do, I do." She smiled at me and continued.

87

"Do you think I dare to go and get us some more drinks?"

"Yes, please, be bold and daring!" I encouraged.

She walked away and returned with our two cups brimming with hot coffee.

"I managed!" Stella joked triumphantly.

"You did, and you were fast too." I commented.

"Yeah sure. Speedy Gonzalez is my name and maybe you should have a look into your notion of speed and time." Stella was not short of a quick reply and seemed to be out of the black whole.

"Maybe I should. Funny you should mention it though. I was just thinking before I got here that it feels as though it's been quite a long time since we last met, and at the same time it feels so recent. Our perception of time really does appear relative, doesn't it?"

"I often think so too. When we feel good and have fun, it has a tendency to pass quickly, and when we don't feel so good or in a painful situation, it's as if the minutes drag. It's the same with the problems that consumed me, until just now when we talked, and all of a sudden they are gone, although nothing has really changed. Not that I complain though." Stella sounded relieved.

"Yes, it's quite amazing how busy we can be with things that have no relevance other than in our minds – and we can spend quite a lot of time on these…illusions." I paused. "Ha, we spend what sometimes feels like forever in illusory black holes, but if we then give them what seems like a moment of scrutiny, they're gone. My God, we humans are something, aren't we?"

"Well, we sure seem to do our best to keep ourselves busy."

"We do. And for the record, about the deck of cards and not getting the instructions that you mentioned…"

"Yes?" Stella inquired curiously.

"The fact is that I don't think there are any for any of us. We often have to learn the hard way, through trial and error, but actually, what we tend to call errors are nothing but experiences from which we learn; if we're astute enough."

"What a bummer. There goes another of my excuses. At the same time, thank goodness we're all explorers on this sometimes challenging path of life."

When I drove back home that evening, my thoughts wandered. Illusions or not, many of us are sometimes pulled into our inner black holes or dark caves, and as Stella and I talked about it on several occasions, when push comes to shove, it seems like we need to accept these emotional valleys if we want to experience the peaks. If we also can relax with – and in – this rollercoaster and maybe even enjoy the ride, then all the better. It cannot always be hunky-dory. With the attitude of allowing and acknowledging the feelings, instead of fighting against them, we may make it an inner adventure rather than a struggle. The missing of someone or something, for example, is something that can feel like a devouring black hole, and yet if we give ourselves the moment to be with it, acknowledge it and sense it, we may also find that behind it there is someone or something that mattered, that was and still is precious. The missing may then bring a feeling of gratitude for having had that experience, that beautiful moment, which then may also lend beauty to the present moment of missing – and longing.

Having reached that conclusion, we also agreed that sometimes we may alleviate the potential heaviness of the perceived darkness by making an effort to do something uplifting, like connecting with a friend, listening to music, dancing, going out into nature, or whatever might be a support, since no one else can do it for us.

Perhaps we also need to give ourselves a reality check. My reality at that point was to park the car and dedicate some time to the children and Donna, holding the opinion that what some people call quality time is often an excuse for a lack of the quantity of the time spent – usually in reference to family. I had better watch out, or I might find myself throwing stones in a glass house.

Chapter 10

Stella Spices Hot Topics

Each spice has its taste
Every colour its nuances
Is there really anyone
Better or worse
Or more beautiful
Than the other?
If we don't compare
Then love is there
Giving joy
Like tulips in the spring

It's strange; when Carl and I were together as a couple, I could not deny that I was quite jealous, and now, even though I would say we are closer than ever and he has his beautiful, younger wife and cute children, I can actually say that I am not. Of course we are not a couple anymore, but nevertheless. Whether Carl would consider himself jealous or not, I could not really tell, but might find out. There are different kinds of jealousy to be explored too, I thought.

"Have you ever been jealous of your wife's or girlfriend's friends? Or your friends for that matter?"
This was something I had been curious about in more general terms for some time, and now I heard myself ask Carl, probably as a representative for men as such, rather than anything else.

"Have I what? How do you mean?" Carl seemed puzzled.

"Well, you know, if you've felt she spends too much time with them, or is too close or open with them, or having too much fun, or whatever; maybe that she doesn't seem to get what she needs from you, so seeks it elsewhere?" I explained.

"Well, as long as it isn't with another man, I'd say it's ok." Carl smiled.

"Sure. But please, would you at least give it some consideration?"

"I will; I already do," Carl assured.

"Good. I'm glad."

"Actually, in my experience, she has tended to spend less and less time with her friends, and as far as I remember, that has been the case with former girlfriends too. Maybe that just says something about me, but it does seem to be the case for many of my friends' wives and girlfriends too. It almost makes me feel guilty – and sometimes really does, since I often take the time to hang out with my friends and do what I like to do. And when I'm with you, she has to bear with me for wanting to spend time with not only a friend, but also an attractive woman, rather than making the effort to get home earlier."

"Ooops…"

For some reason I felt a little abashed. If I had been in Donna's place, the chances are that I probably would have been jealous.

"Yeah, ooops!"

"And when the two of you see friends together, is it more often your friends or hers?"

Maybe this was a different subject, but the way I had made the association, it apparently was connected.

"Ehmm...that's not obvious, and it doesn't happen every week, nor even every month, but I'd say it's more often with her original friends, or our neighbours and friends we have got to know via the children."

"So, you see your friends on your own more often than the two of you socialise together, and she usually doesn't see her friends, or do what used to be her 'things' as much as you do?" I tried to summarise.

"Right," Carl confirmed.

"And you said that this sometimes makes you feel guilty?"

I started to feel like a Gallup survey questioner, but Carl did not seem to mind.

"Yes, and to be honest, if I perhaps stretch it a little, I can also see how I have somehow ended up in a metaphorical bubble with girlfriends, and when that bubble has eventually felt too small, I've felt that I had to break out of it, thus breaking up the relationship," Carl said frankly.

"Like with us?"

"Yes, I think we could say that was one part of it. Maybe it's a paradox, but I can see that I haven't always been particularly encouraging in terms of my girlfriends seeing their friends, or us seeing them with their partners." Carl looked pensive.

"Well, I'd say I remember that one. I was actually afraid you'd leave me if I did – and, speaking of paradoxes, that happened anyway," I smiled.

"Yeah...and I was probably grumpy more than once too, if you felt like that," Carl acknowledged.

"Well, there are always two in a relationship, so it's only fair to say we both played our part."

"Thank you." Carl looked at me and we both smiled.

"But I still find it kind of intriguing, or at least interesting," I carried on.

"What?"

"Now I'm generalising, since that makes it a little easier and more convenient, but how so many of us women have this tendency to give up so many of our friends and activities when boyfriends come into the picture."

"I think we can go on with that generalisation, even though we could probably find evidence to the contrary too."

"No doubt; no rules without exceptions, right?"

We both smiled again; there seemed to be something here we both wanted to look into.

"If only we could see what we are doing - and not doing for that matter." I paused.

"Yes? You have me curious."

"Really? Well, let's see…I don't know, but probably all of us, men and women, share this longing to love, to give and receive love." I felt like I was stating the obvious.

"I think that is pretty close to a given."

"And we women at least are usually so single-minded and focus entirely on THE relationship and THE partner – and of course on our children, if we have any; albeit in another way with them."

"I love these generalisations, but yes, and men too, sometimes, if I may add," Carl emphasised.

"Ok, I couldn't argue too much with that, could I?"

"It probably wouldn't be all that easy anyway," Carl laughed.

"Probably not. So, we seem to believe that we have to economise also with our love, that we cannot spend it on too many, as if we are afraid it will run out.

However, when it comes to the mathematics of love, the love we feel for our children is a great teacher, wouldn't you agree?"

"I sure hope I do."

"With them it becomes so obvious, which probably every parent with more than one child has experienced. No matter how much you feel like your heart is bursting with love for your first child, there is room for just as much love for a second child, and a third, and a fourth."

The fact that I had not become a mother did not imply that I could not see this as another kind of given and had seen it among family and friends.

"Yes! And I do! Agree, I mean – and love my children." Carl the father awakened.

"That's a relief." I smiled at Carl, who was grinning.

"Maybe you've also noticed that the same actually goes for love in general. The more you love; the more love you give, the more love is there for you to give. Moreover, the more you give, the more you receive."

"Ahh, maybe this is what old John Maynard Keynes had noticed and thought it applied to money too, with his 'Spend your way to prosperity' theory. Sorry, I couldn't help myself. But yes, I agree again, love actually does seem to be self-regenerating." Carl the economist woke up too.

"Good, since that's kind of the point here." I laughed, and continued. "So, coming back to the bubble-syndrome; if we, and now I'm letting that women generalisation bloom, dare to really see, love and support other women and friends, our need to love a man, and that one man - or woman for that matter - will not be the only target. Thus, we will presumably not be so suffocating, so demanding, so limiting and even frightening, as men sometimes perceive us, when we are in a relationship." I exhaled deeply.

"This sounds like a double-win, at least," Carl suggested.

"Yes, I also think it would be. The sad part is that instead there's often so much envy, jealousy and competition between us women," I confessed.

"I've noticed that more than once."

"I bet you have. It is such a pity to me and, sure, I've caught myself in it more than once too. I don't know, but maybe it goes back to the time when women really were dependent on their men for their survival and couldn't afford to lose them. Maybe that's also where this need to be needed – that most of us seem to have – stems from?"

"You ask me; I'm a man, remember. But it does sound quite plausible to me."

"Today, we're not really dependent on a man for our survival and value as a human being, I mean. Yet, sometimes I wonder…" My words trailed off.

"Wonder what?" Carl urged.

"How come our society is still so based on people not being individuals, but couples?"

"Do you have an example?" Carl asked.

"Take, for instance, when you want to book a holiday, or a charter trip. I'd say that from my observations, at least nine times out of ten, the so-called number of people travelling is pre-set on two. And if you want to travel charter, the price quoted is always for sharing a double room. If you want to travel alone or single, you'd better be prepared to pay a substantial premium. If a restaurant has an offer stating that children under a certain age can eat for free, or at a reduced price, there is usually the precondition that there must be at least two fully paying adults."

"Even though households with single adults are now the majority in most places. It really is a bit strange. But yes, the couple – and preferably married – still seems to be the norm. And with two children," Carl added.

"Maybe that's one of the major contributing factors to why we women still seem to find it difficult to really enjoy each other, and to keep our 'I-part', as soon as a relationship is in play," I speculated.

"Could be, since it's perhaps not quite the same thing for us men. And yet, there are single men too."

"There are, but somehow you seem to last longer; not in terms of average life-span, but on the market, the best-before date, or however you want to put it."

"Now you just have to be more specific, Stella. I'm curious," Carl teased.

"I had a feeling you would say something like that, although I'm quite sure you know what I mean."

I looked at him, observed that he would probably be considered by many to be at a safe distance from his best-before date, and continued.

"Ok, for you it's much more accepted, or even admired, to have a young or much younger girlfriend or wife, and we can probably both recognise that a mature man more often has more money and/or power and status than a mature woman, which also seems to be part of the attraction between the older man and the younger woman. It doesn't seem to be the equivalent case for most women – with a few exceptions to the rule of course."

"We could probably say that the roots of this go way back," Carl suggested.

"Yes, and the rules we still basically play by, were set by men."

"Rules that have become once again a given and, in general, we men are still usually the ones in the position of power and we don't see much reason to change them, do we?"

"Well, why would you want to change them? There are indeed some vested interests here, but sure, things have happened and still do, so the playground is changing, albeit in small steps. That's inevitable and life means change, whether we like it or not."

"Yeah, and since you mentioned babies and we're kind of into the subject, what do you think about parental leave and how to divide it?"

Carl's question touched, or maybe scratched, the political agenda.

"Now, that's another hot potato." I looked at him and wondered what this turn could imply.

"I know; that's why I'm curious about what you think." Carl looked back at me somewhat expectantly.

"Ha, ha, yeah, experience talking, right? Perhaps you wanting to change the subject?"

I could not help but find the situation rather funny.

"Experience or not, I'm sure you have thought about it, and I would like to hear your opinion," Carl insisted.

"I guess I have to admit; yes, I have given it some thought and talked about it with friends." I hesitated a little, knowing that this could be a touch subject probably also for Carl. "Well, ok, neck out then. Having a child entails responsibilities...for both parents of course. If the child is the focus of attention and not the desires or ambitions of either parent – or what we call society, at least short-term, which seems to be the term in most areas these days – these responsibilities look a little different for the mother and father respectively, at least in the beginning, right?"

Carl nodded and I went on.

"From what I've learnt and seen, looking to biology and psychology etc., and most parents and experts would agree, during the early stages of a child's life, its direct need for the mother is bigger than that for the father, since breastfeeding is nature's gift and original way of nurturing, taking care of, connecting with, and protecting the baby. In addition, the baby spent around nine months in its mother's womb, literally being a part of her. Even when everything goes well enough and the baby is healthy, time is still obviously needed for both of them – especially the baby – to tune into the two separate beings they are. If the parents are normally healthy, this is the natural way, how nature or existence created us, I dare say."

I paused and asked myself how we had come to question this fundamental need in a so-called civilised modern society.

"Yes, this is basically a fact of life, or perhaps we might be inclined to say 'was' these days."

Carl expressed what I had just thought. With modern science and modern life, we have also found ways to bypass nature, to the great joy of many. However, without judging, I just hope we will also realise that it may have consequences that are not always so clear in the immediate and the outer, as well as the inner, and that it will probably have to be dealt with a bit more elaborately and with more consciousness, even though not everything can be foreseen.

"Mmm, it is a bit strange, at least to me. Breastfeeding is just one, although perhaps the most obvious aspect. The connection and interplay between the mother and child is also crucial for our brain's development, for how, what and who we become, how we feel about ourselves and others, how we deal with different kinds of stress. It is a time when a significant part of the foundation of our abilities, personality and attitudes in life is created. So if nature allows you to be, and you choose to become a parent, you also get what some people call the world's most important job. So, as a mother, during the first year or so at least, you are most likely, or hopefully, inclined to put your eventual 'market career' on hold, because a new life has been given to you to take care of. That's more or less biology.

"After the first year – 18 months or so, I'd say it's beautiful if the father can also stay home to allow the natural bonding to develop between the child and him. Of course, there is a need for the father before that, in different ways, but from then on the direct need for the father grows. Basically, I would argue that a child has the right to both parents, if possible, and biologically is sprung from and needs both of them; hopefully, two loving, caring and responsible ones. Today, the reality may look different for different families in different places and has to be worked out as well as it can be, according to the circumstances and personal priorities." I took a sip of water and looked at Carl. "So, an opinion as of today."

"Ok, I get it and won't argue against it, since I can recognise most of it from my own experience as a

100

father and partner. Luckily, I'd say, we're not into cloning yet."

Carl nodded his head slowly, as if to emphasise what he had just said, before he continued.

"Have you noticed that babies often look quite a lot like the father? When I look at pictures of mine and of me as a baby it's quite amazing, even if that changes as they grow; luckily in my case, I must say! Apparently, that's nature's way of convincing the man that he is the father, in case there are doubts. Anyway, what we have to remember, is that in far too many cases and countries, parents don't really have the option of staying at home with the child for more than a couple of months, or even weeks, unless they are quite well off financially."

"Yes. I have friends in different corners of the world who had to face leaving their young babies to return to work; something they had felt awful about, yet still felt that they had to do; that it was 'normal'."

"That is sad and has become another fact of life," Carl sighed.

"Very sad to me too. I'm afraid we haven't seen the full consequences of this and our modern lifestyles on our children yet. Then again, I'm quite sure we can assume that most parents do the best they can and want what they perceive to be the best for their children."

"No, we probably haven't seen the full consequences. The question is, do 'we' really want to? At the same time, I guess that all eras have their different challenges, right? We also see many kinds of families, 'solutions', and ways to cope and, like you said, basically we all do our best given the circumstances and we deserve to be respected for that."

Carl's questions and conclusions were pertinent.

101

"No doubt. Only time will tell, but hopefully we do want to and will do something about it. More than likely, we'll have to, in some way."

When I heard myself, I realised I could not say whether I was being optimistic, pessimistic, or realistic. Not that it really mattered. Time would tell and had probably already started to do so, considering the prevalence of children with ADHD and similar diagnoses; again probably not a politically correct observation. It's as if we as human beings have not kept up with the society we have created – and maybe cannot, since parts of our brain and nervous system still function the way they did even before we evolved into homo sapiens.

"It's also kind of interesting with this gender and equality debate. Did you know that some people even want to go as far as to stop calling their children he or she, and instead use a more neutral pronoun; not 'it' though…yet."

Carl sounded as appalled as I sometimes felt about this.

"Yes, I heard about it. It may of course be helpful in general when we don't know if we are talking about a he or a she, or wish to remain neutral, and it can be practical sometimes to write or say 'the' instead of 'he or she'. Still, the perceived need behind it is somehow sad to me and I cannot help but wonder why it seems to appear so abhorrent to admit that we are different in many ways. Of course, we should be neutral in the sense of one not being worth more than the other, but I mean if we were all the same, that would be kind of boring, wouldn't it? And not particularly dynamic."

"Yes, to me that's the springing point – that we are different, yet of equal value and importance – and where we would need to do something. Now we're touching on another big subject. Is it ok if we save it for another time? I'm afraid I don't have time today go into that the way I'd like to."

Carl looked at his watch and obviously felt the urge to go home to his family.

"I have the children waiting and the more we talk about life and children, the more I realise how precious and short childhood is and how much I would like to take advantage of being with them and creating good memories, rather than 'should haves'."

"That sounds beautiful to me, so yes, let's save that other topic."

Apparently Carl could be jealous, like most of us. I have heard some people argue about what I would call 'ordinary jealousy', stating that it simply shows that you are truly in love. I am not so sure about that. Jealousy can exist in other kinds of relationships too, like friendships. What seems more obvious, however, is that jealousy is a sign or symptom of insecurity, of fear of being perceived as not good enough to the other, and of being rejected. A lesson to be learned is probably to start by not rejecting oneself, which I have often found is easier said than done.

Maybe the theory of 'opposites attract' also plays a role in terms of jealousy. The other has something I am attracted to, that I 'want' – and which thereby might also make me insecure, since on some level I believe I do not have it, and perhaps I am unfamiliar with those characteristics. Relating with a partner – and polarity in the outer, in addition to our inner polarities, whereby the male and female sides we all possess play a part – that is the norm, to become 'one' with another and in that way maybe complement and even complete

103

ourselves and each other. Maybe that in itself implies even jealousy as normal, since if we end up without a partner, that is often considered odd and even shameful, which we learn from very early on, even though single households in fact are quite common today.

If we do end up without a partner, what do we do? What did I do? For a good while a part of me was looking for one, wanting to be 'normal'. I kissed a number of frogs and when the transformation from a frog into a prince did not happen, I began to examine the reality of my situation, to look into myself, and realised I did not mind being alone.

Relating with myself; I even like it and have come to like myself – at least most of the time. The assumed need for sex is not really a drive anymore; as enjoyable as it may be, it could be that sex is one thing that the body moves down on the priority list when it is focused on dealing with what is more essential to functioning and getting by day to day, rather than the survival of the species. Or perhaps I've had my fair share in this life and it is basically over and done with? Or bypassed? Or paused? Or maybe that is just another protection? Who knows?

The need for closeness, touch, pleasure and wellbeing I can fulfil with friends, by having massages and by enjoying the senses in other ways, not least by meditating, as strange as it may sound to someone who has not yet had that experience. It sometimes seems as though being single is more of a problem to others, often in a relationship, than it usually is to me – although it sometimes is to me too. A friend once suggested that maybe they are just envious. I feel that it is more likely out of care and loving concern.

Be that as it may, whatever life situations we end up in and whatever choices we make, we will never know how it would have turned out had we made other choices. Sometimes I may miss being with someone when I am not and at other times I may want to be alone when I am with someone. Sometimes I would like to share more of this life with someone and life seems empty without a partner, but sometimes life is abundantly full. These talks with Carl gave me a feeling of how my life could have been had I gone down that path. He had shown me some of the things I may miss out on, but equally, the many things and experiences I get instead. So far.

Chapter 11

Carl Ends Up in a Mystery Where Ghosts May Not Be Such Ghastly Hosts

Tell me
What you know
Nothing
And that would be all

"Do you believe in ghosts? Or rather, in life after this?"

Stella had just had a bite of her chocolate mousse cake and tasted it with closed eyes when I asked the question. She slowly swallowed the cake, opened her eyes, and looked at me.

"May I ask why you ask?"

"Yes, you may." I smiled. "And may I just add that I really enjoy watching you when you are eating, what you would probably call, a good chocolate cake."

She laughed.

"Well, obviously I enjoy it too. This one is actually very rich in taste without being too sweet or bitter or heavy. It might become a favourite. So, why?"

"It's been on my mind for a while, after a strange experience with a candle one morning. It made me wonder what had happened and I didn't have my usual rational explanation. So I'm curious to hear what you think."

"What happened with the candle?"

"Well, on a chest-of-drawers in the bedroom, we have a candle holder with a candle. It was lit the evening before and I blew it out before going to bed. When I woke up in the morning it was burning."

"And no one else had lit it?"

"No. I asked Donna, and she said she hadn't. And the children couldn't have done it."

"Actually, I've had a very similar experience."

"You have?"

"Yes. It happened a few years ago. And, who knows? We can't really, can we? Considering the fact that the range of frequencies and vibrations man can actually see and hear is very limited, there might very well be something there that we cannot perceive with our senses, and as of today and as far as I know, also not technically measure or register. Well, some people claim they do; I don't know if I want to call it ghosts, but maybe that's what they are and they might just be around, their energy lingering, until they feel ready to move on."

"Move on?"

"Yes. Not that I know whereto of course; next body, next life, 'heaven' or 'hell' as some might call it. You also mentioned life after this, didn't you? I guess the two must be connected somehow and as I understood it, you do too?"

"Yeah, I guess I do. It's almost funny; I cannot really say that I never see the world in black or white anymore, but I can say that my perspectives have broadened, that I do see that there are a lot of grey areas, not to mention colour. Like now, hearing myself say that I more or less believe in ghosts and life after this is far removed from my old convictions."

"Good for you! I think..." She smiled and had another bite of the chocolate cake. "And this cake really is delicious by the way."

"I'm sure of that one. About the grey…probably. I mean, there is rarely, if ever, any single or simple answer to any question or issue. On the contrary, every issue seems to have different aspects, or perspectives, or layers, or dimensions, or whatever we prefer to call them; most or all unconscious as I guess you would agree to call them."

"Mmm…" She was still enjoying the cake.

"And if we take you as an example, I seem to recall that we almost touched on this subject once, when I asked about the diseases, didn't we?"

"Yes, we did, kind of, if you mean what I think you mean. So, if we look at the diagnoses, 'the diseases', I have a feeling this could apply in many cases, but just to simplify it, let's say it's about the infamous 'me, myself, and I'."

"Please."

I had a quick glance at my watch; still time. I had a feeling Stella and I could get quite involved in this.

"So, the one who becomes sick, or seriously ill, let's say; now, what I might call the 'I', for instance, could see it as something that just happens to happen, a misfortune, rather random, maybe caused by a virus, or a genetic predisposition and thereby I would in some sense victimise myself. Or, depending on the circumstances when the first symptoms appeared, it could be seen as the body's reaction to those circumstances; like a reaction to a divorce, to yet another rejection, another love that did not get to blossom and bear fruit, or maybe to being fired, or someone close dying, since scientists seem to agree that our immune system becomes weakened on occasions like that. This makes us more vulnerable to

108

'inner attacks' that are actually more or less constantly happening."

"Yes, I've read some articles about that too."

"It could also be seen as a defence strategy – unconscious of course – where I slowly kill myself before anyone can come close enough and kill me. Maybe not literally kill me, but I think you know what I mean and we touched on it before."

"Ok, I think I do. However, the benefits of such a strategy could be discussed, you know."

"Tell me about it." She smiled and went on. "Here comes another one. One dimension of it could also be that it is an expression of a huge love, usually towards a mother and/or father, and of the longing to feel a connection with them. Or, it could be a 'task', a destiny, which a sensitive being can be given or take on, in order to make something visible, or to atone for something on a soul level in the family system."

"Wow, this sounds a bit complicated, if not surreal to me, but then again, children really do anything for their parents, even if it's sometimes, or maybe very often, not clear to either party."

I almost got goosebumps when a few situations with the kids came to mind.

"Indeed; parents would usually do anything for their children, although that is perhaps clearer. There's more. In some sense, it could also be seen as turning my energy against myself, since expressing it in any other way was on some level perceived as too dangerous or as not allowed. Or, and most likely, a mix of all of them or parts of these aspects, perhaps together with other not yet disclosed ones. Who knows? I don't, but looking at it from these different perspectives has made me much more at ease with the

109

diseases, and not least the dimension of seeing it as an expression of unconscious love."

"Yes, it feels like that from where I see you too. By the way, why do you point that dimension out?" I was curious.

"Oh, I guess that was in the moment, but since I did, it presumably has its reasons. Why? Well, like I've said before, I have had difficulties accepting myself for almost as long as I can remember, and the physical conditions have not made it any easier. Seeing and feeling what my family field showed in so-called family or systemic constellations, where this act of unconscious or blind love somehow became visible and 'clear', were very strong experiences. They made me realise that this also showed a powerful love, which is a part of me at least as much as the diseases. If I continued fighting against these physical conditions, I'd reject and deny not only them, but also my parents, me, other people and, above all, this love and this incredible capability to love, which is there in me – in all of us for that matter. Love that no longer only has to express itself unconsciously. So, I think you could say it has helped me to find the courage to tell people who are important to me that I love them. And you are one of them." Stella looked at me, a little shyly.

"Mmmm, beautiful. I'm glad and appreciate that. And what's that family constellation thing you mentioned?"

"Well, in short, it's a method, or a tool, or work, or whatever you call it, by a German therapist called Bert Hellinger. I think I've mentioned him before, if you remember, where you let representatives, or symbols if you don't do it in a group, tap into what he calls the knowing field of your family system, and then you let

110

things unfold and see what happens. It's difficult to explain; it needs to be experienced to do it justice and many find it magical."

"It really does sound intriguing; please let me know should the occasion arise to experience it. I would love to be there."

I also made a mental note to google this Hellinger.

"Sure, I will." She looked happy.

"So, coming back to ghosts and the next life; what we may pick up from different energies lurking, what we do, how we live our days in this life, not only influence how we feel about this life, but probably will influence our next life too then, would you agree?"

"Hmm, well, yes, in a way I suppose I would."

"Then that would also mean that how we've spent former lives affects this life, right? I mean, here we have the Eastern concept or idea, or what they call 'karma', don't we?"

"Yes."

"Karma or not, do you also think we can have what we might call 'past life experiences'?" I really felt I was walking on thin ice here.

"You mean like in dreams, or visions, or sensations, or maybe even symptoms?"

"Well, I didn't think of symptoms, but now that you mention it, yeah, why not?"

"We keep answering each other with new questions." Stella smiled. "I like that. And yes, I have to say that in some sense I do. I might even stretch it as far as to say that it has sometimes occurred to me that it could affect – or maybe explain – some of my behaviours today."

"Ok. Could you explain that a bit more, please? Any examples?"

"Yeah, well...I'll try anyway. Of course, I can't say that I have facts; it's more like different experiences, body sensations, images and feelings that I've had in different situations over the years, which have given me a lingering impression that something in me has experienced things before being in this body. Let's say, for example, that I've had a gruesome experience in a past life, as a consequence to something I had done or was accused of doing, and this really caused suffering, to me and possibly also to others."

"Yes?"

"Maybe, on some level I carry a memory of that, which today makes me avoid doing or acting in the way that caused suffering back then, even if I am a different person now, living under different circumstances and in a very different society."

"Interesting, but why not; I mean, we carry all kinds of memories in our system, otherwise we wouldn't function or even be here, would we?"

"No, probably not. So, coming back to your question, I can't really say that I do, and I also can't say that I don't."

Stella exhaled and seemed to relax a bit more, as if she had been hesitating about my reaction.

"It's strange, we have all these capacities, abilities, imprints and memories, yet still we do not know. Luckily, we always end up with a mystery."

"Yes!" Stella agreed.

"This reminds me of that quote from Osho you've mentioned."

"You're referring to what seems to be our favourite, 'Life is not a problem to be solved, it is a mystery to be lived' – and enjoyed?"

"Yes, that is a good one."

"It is, and we seem to need to be reminded again and again."

"We do, so it's good that we do it then; remind each other, I mean." I winked at her.

"Yes, and rather than starting worrying about the next life, perhaps it would be a good thing to see to it that we really do live and enjoy this life, in this body, before we leave it; and if we do, then we probably have neither time nor reason to worry about what comes after or what may have been before…"

"Ha, ha, yes, good point. I'm also happy to enjoy this day with you."

"Me too. And I have a feeling there will be more to be explored and enjoyed."

Karma. Past lives. This life. The things we do, or do not do and the people we meet. Some stay on for longer, others just appear and disappear; most we don't even register unless something happens and, not least after this discussion with Stella, I had the feeling that they all affect us more than we might imagine, and maybe all for a reason. A reason to learn something, to grow, to love, to…who knows? Another mystery.

Chapter 12

Stella is High on Life on the Ground

A trinity, holy may be
Body, mind, soul
Feeling
Thinking
Knowing
Being one whole

"What have you been up to? You look…unusually fresh and lively somehow, if you don't mind my saying so. I've understood that some people, especially women, don't like that description – fresh I mean – and I never understood why," Carl postulated, as he approached the table in our favourite corner.

"I don't mind. I even like it, so thank you. Maybe the 'unusually' part could make me wonder how I usually look though!" I teased him a little.

"Oh come on! I meant it as a compliment!" Carl emitted a theatrical sigh.

"Ok, well, I just came back from my little haven, so it must be that," I grinned.

"I gather you had a good time, then?"

"Yes! The weather was just lovely and that's always a huge advantage in my world, so I spent quite some time outdoors, took a few little walks, practised some gardening – weeding, planting, fertilising and watering, you know. I often just love doing as much of it as I can, which is not so much if one compares, but anyway."

Thinking of the weekend brought back the feeling of relaxation in action, albeit slow and small, and I liked that.

"Yes, I like it too, in reasonable doses, although it usually implies some digging, lawn-mowing and more cumbersome chores when I do it. Perhaps I should get one of those robot-mowers." Carl looked pleased with this idea.

"Maybe you should. Well, I didn't have so much of that this time. It really felt so good to let whatever I did take its time and I really found myself...in awe, I'd say, of the beautiful, fresh greenery – the flowers, the trees, and even the weeds. I marvelled at the insects, the little foal nearby and everything that is there, that works and can 'do' so many things, without knowing or asking 'how' or 'why'; just like us really, if we stick to the body. I can only describe it as a feeling of unity, that all life is sacred."

When I am in that space, I find it difficult even to squash a mosquito.

"Yeah, otherwise I'd say we really do have a tendency to question, to improve and whatever, but you sure seem to have been – and still are – in touch with something...something great."

"Yes, I almost felt like a child, at least what I would call a childlike wonder and joy. It was one of these occasions where I really could feel this vibrating energy inside, as if every cell was alive, vibrant."

The sensation came back to me the moment I started describing it.

"Well they are, aren't they? Sorry, I'm just envious."

"Well, you should be!"

We both laughed at this.

"You know, all this life, all this wisely arranged energy, all these miracles!"

The weekend had made me high on life.

"It's like we not only live in one of all the universes, moreover we all have a universe within us, with 'our essence' as the sun or centre in our inner solar system. The sun's always there, but sometimes it's obscured by clouds. We have learnt that the weather and seasons change, that nothing is permanent, which may open up our eyes to all its beauty in different shapes. Also, our inner clouds are sometimes many – grey, dense, sometimes few, sheer, light and sometimes even non-existent! Nothing is permanent. Speaking of non-permanence, when I touch a space and feeling like that, maybe I could call it 'flow' or totality, the notion of time also shifts. It's as if time stands still and at the same time passes very quickly, almost as though it disappears."

I stopped and looked around, sensing that maybe others would react to my getting a bit carried away. Anyway, that would actually be their problem rather than mine; I had done nothing but describe what had come to me during those days, maybe a bit livelier than most people around us. I noticed the familiar fear of standing out in a bad way, or of being too much, flashing through my system. Then the metaphor of those fears being like meteorites in my atmosphere followed, and I began to smile.

"You really had a good weekend!"

"Yes, I told you. Do you want more, or was that already more than enough?" I felt I had better ask.

"Are you out of your mind? I wouldn't want to miss it." Carl appeared genuinely eager to hear some more.

"Ha, ha, I hope so; out of my mind I mean. Ok. So, I cannot run away from the clouds within me – or within us. Hopefully, I can make them disperse, or wait for them to disappear when needed."

"Hopefully," he smiled, "but how?"

"Here we go; one of these human 'why's'."

"Ooops…"

"Yeah, what would you say about noticing them without giving them so much attention, followed by courage if facing strong emotions; patience and presence to remember that the situation is probably not as bad as the thought; acceptance since what was, was, and what is, is; and maybe action like 'bringing in some light'?" I asked.

"Could probably come handy, but my goodness, that would take something."

"Well, yes, I don't know. I have heard so many times that the answers are within me; I just need to listen and sometimes a part of me has said 'Yes!' and sometimes a part of me has just wanted to scream 'Shut up,' or at least tell me where and how, you know. So, the conclusion then must be that I just need to listen, do it more often, make it a new or stronger habit, practice, and then maybe one day what I long to know might reveal itself to me."

I made the gesture of opening my palms as to receive something.

"Well, it sounds to me like you found some answers already this weekend, if not before."

"Hopefully, you're right. I probably did, although maybe I can't really hear, see, or grasp them yet." I shook my head.

"If I didn't know better, I'd say that it sounds almost as though you had a religious experience," Carl suggested.

"Funny that you mention it, because I was thinking the same thing myself. I mean, it's twofold in a way, since somehow I feel more 'religious' than ever in the sense of awe and wonder before existence, life, God, or whatever you like to call it, yet at the same time I feel farther away from religion, church and priests."

"Well, the church does do some good."

"I know it does and I'm not against it. I'd even say that there are some Christian messages that are quite valid in their original sense, most likely in other religions too," I admitted.

"Like?"

"Like for example the so-called golden rule."

"You mean the one about doing to others what you would like to have done to you, or however the saying goes."

Carl proved that he knew at least one biblical quote.

"That very one. I don't know what you think, but to me it really seems to hold true that whatever we put into others' lives will come back into our own; that life somehow echoes what we say and do."

"I agree and maybe the easiest and most obvious example is that when you smile at someone, you usually get a smile back." He smiled at me and I smiled back.

"See!"

"Yes, how could I not agree to that one? So let's keep smiling at as many people as possible."

"Ha, ha, our new religion."

"Yes, as long as it is not a fake smile, this one may even bring some laughter! Or maybe 'fake it 'til you make it' works too?"

"Finally, let's try, the more the better!" Carl beamed at me and added, "Also, another twist to that golden rule could be to do unto others what they would like to be done to them; I mean, shifting the focus from yourself to the other. At least sometimes."

"A good point my dear, although that may take more communication, since mind-reading is not really that obvious. I don't know if this is relevant, but coming back to nature, reality and all its miracles and effects, it struck me not too long ago how far from it many of us seem to have ended up."

"How do you mean?"

"Well, we're so busy trying to create copies of it, that we tend to forget the original, the real."

"I assume you're not referring to Coke and Pepsi here?" Carl asked dryly.

"Ha, ha, no, I'm not. But one example in that area would be all the sweets and candy with artificial fruit flavours that are supposed to taste like real strawberries, bananas, pineapples, pears or whatever."

"With so much sugar and chemical stuff added, kids and adults no longer think that the real thing tastes like the real thing, which would be the strawberry jelly or marshmallow," Carl added.

"It's almost tragic. Another aspect of that is how modern agriculture has altered the nutritional value and taste, so we cannot really compare an orange or apple or potato of today with those of say 40-50 years ago."

119

When I first heard this, I was ready to buy land and start organic farming, but something in me was a bit more realistic than that.

"Yeah, but that's a different story, which also has other aspects, so let's save that one because that's a biggie, since I'm quite convinced you have another pertinent example of your observations." Carl's brow furrowed slightly.

"Ha, ha, yes! Are you trying to flatter me into something or what? By the way, I like it when you frown like that."

"I do? You do? No, I'm not trying anything; I'm just curious."

"Ok, if you say so. Another example then?"

"Yes, please, give me the bait," he laughed.

"3D."

"3D?" Carl repeated and looked surprised.

"Yes, 3D. We no longer seem to be satisfied with a movie on a screen; now we prefer the movie projecting out of the screen and behind it, and…"

"Ha, ha, maybe that was the ultimate vision of the first movie makers; not only moving pictures, but pictures moving to you."

"Yes, maybe. My point here though would be that some people seem to think of the 3D-animation effect as the real thing and then when they go into a garden or nature, they are perplexed that nature actually IS in 3D; that if you don't watch out, the branches of a tree actually do point in all directions and can poke you if you walk into them."

I had been astonished more than once by people referring to this.

"Trees attack! You're right; it's actually quite funny in a way. The real world, out there at their feet, waiting to be discovered – if only they'd look away from the screen. On the screen note, let me just add the 'blind' use of GPS, which seems to induce oblivion to what the roads, streets and signs actually show. It's surprising how many times I've heard about people driving in all kinds of directions and even into trees and houses because they followed that little gadget." He shook his head and we both laughed.

"A treasure box like no other. Nature I mean."

As useful and handy a GPS might be, I felt I had better clarify what I meant.

"Yeah…" Carl replied, hesitantly.

"What? You seem to be miles away and now it's my turn to be curious."

"Well, I just remembered one of those treasures…"

"Aha?" Now he really had me hooked.

"One day this spring, when the trees were budding and it had been raining, I could see the raindrops resting on the buds of the trees along the road, even while I was driving. That, together with a beautiful soft light and the formations of the different layers of the clouds was just so amazingly beautiful."

As he recalled it, Carl's eyes somehow reflected that picture to me.

"I think I can imagine and there's always something to be amazed by, if only we are open to it."

"Yeah. Life. Nature. The original and best…and what you said about childlike wonder. Now I remember so many times with the children, their amazement with more or less everything. One of their first words, for example, is 'Look!' and they point to something, or bring something and look so happy about it."

"Mmmm; there are so many things we try to, and need to, teach children. At the same time, I think it would be a great gift to all if we also remembered and acknowledged that it actually goes both ways; what great teachers they are to us too."

On the teaching note, I remembered a quote from Byron Katie, at least that is whom I think it was, who said that 'we are all good teachers, but the question is what we teach', since what we may think we teach and what others actually learn from us might be two different things. Children tend to do what we do rather than what we tell them to do. That, too, feels like a good one to remember and from which to learn.

Chapter 13

Carl Recalls the Call

Entering my temple
Coming home
I find the light inside
And recognise it in all
Letting go of rocks
Diamonds abide

For some odd reason, I called Stella one morning. She was surprised and who could blame her; it had been years and years since we had last talked. My lame excuse was to ask her about hotels in a place I remembered she used to visit. She had not married, had no children and seemed to be single. She sounded happy. She told me she would not be around if I went there at the time I had planned to, because she would be on holiday elsewhere for the whole summer. One of the things she would do was to go somewhere and meditate – for weeks! When I said I had not had a holiday in years, she remarked that we all have our priorities and asked if, in years to come, I thought I would appreciate the fact that I chose to work that much, instead of spending time with my wife and children. I reluctantly admitted that she had a point there.

Stella did congratulate me on establishing my own business, since that was my dream when we were together. Well, it had obviously taken some work and still did. I asked if she would consider sending me a postcard and, if so, to address it to the office to avoid any unnecessary discord at home. She did not promise anything, which was actually something of a surprise to me.

They say curiosity killed the cat, but I became curious about this meditation thing she talked about, so I asked her about it – and luckily I am not a cat. It is strange, but I still remember that conversation and many others with her so clearly, almost as if we had just hung up. As with most things, there seem to be more ways to do it than you think and, in the case of meditation, to not just sit with your legs crossed and your eyes closed and repeat a mantra. Apparently, she got into it some years ago.

"You know, it's a bit like dear old Frost said…"

"Who?"

"Robert Frost, the American poet. Don't you remember your American literature classes?" Stella asked rhetorically.

"I never took it, or if I did, I've forgotten."

"Really? Anyway, it's a bit like in that poem of his; I think it's called 'The Road Not Taken', where two roads diverged in a wood. Like him, I could maybe say I took the one less travelled by and that that has made all the difference to me," Stella more or less quoted.

"And by that you want to say?"

"I don't know if I want to say anything particular, but you asked."

"Sorry, please go ahead; I want to hear more," I urged.

"Well, it's just that, to me, the road or path with meditation and what I might call working on myself was pretty unknown territory, and it has given me something I didn't have before, or rather, didn't realise I had," Stella explained.

"So what is this 'it'?"

"It is like nothing really."

"You make me smile."

"I'm smiling too," she said.

"I know; I could kind of hear that. So you keep on doing this meditation thing because it gives you nothing. Come on, I thought you were smarter than that!"

"Maybe I was…" I could hear her smiling again, then her giggling. She continued.

"And this nothing is really a good thing to me; it's like a new flavour, a new quality of life, an emptiness filled with space."

"You do sound happy."

I had noted a new tone in her voice, which I found appealing.

"I do? Well, basically I am. Of course life has its ups and downs and I do have my occasional down moments, you know, but I guess we all do and they are needed too."

"Know what?"

The way she had said it for some reason did not sound like the usual 'you know'.

"Oh, I forgot; of course you don't know. I developed some physical challenges years ago, and treatments and losing bodily functions can be tough sometimes. As you know, I used to want kids and a family, or at least I thought I did. Sometimes, although not so much anymore, sadness has been there – and anger – but then I allowed it to be there, felt it, watched it, explored it and what was behind it and expressed it in a responsible way. Eventually, I feel that everything is actually ok the way it is. Sorry, I didn't mean to pour all that onto you just like that, after all this time," Stella apologised, which to me was not necessary.

"Is it serious? I mean, the illness; is it serious?"

"The doctors have made a number of diagnoses and some of them are pretty serious."

"What is it?" I wanted to know.

"Some autoimmune and neurological stuff that can affect and basically destroy all organs and tissue."

"Oh... damn...I wish it hadn't happened to you of all people."

"Thanks, but why do you say that? You just told me I sounded happy and I said I am."

"Yes, you do. It's just me. I'm really happy that you are happy despite all of it."

"I'm even happier now that I made you happy, since you didn't sound very happy earlier."

We both laughed.

"You're great. How could I ever have broken up with you?"

"Yes, how could you? Actually I'm kind of glad you did." She laughed again.

"What? It sure as hell didn't seem like it at the time."

I almost felt hurt, however irrational that may seem.

"No, I know, not back then, but who knows how happy I'd have been sitting at home with the kids on a beautiful weekend like this while you're busy at work," Stella joked.

"Touché!"

"And I have a good life. Not the expected Smith-version with a 9-to-5 job, sorry, 24-7 job, husband, children, house, Volvo station-wagon or SUV, dog and summer house, but one with…"

"Is there something wrong with that? And by the way, we don't have a dog."

I could not help but interrupt. Obviously she had touched a sore spot there and I wouldn't mention the dog we had had.

"No, of course not! That's not what I'm saying. I'm just trying to say that there are different ways of living and none necessarily better or worse than the other; just different, like we all are different…and the same," she tried to explain.

"What was that? The last thing you mumbled?"

"I was just saying that we are all different and at the same time, the same."

"That's a bit contradictory to me. How do you mean?" I asked.

"Oh, I don't mean anything particular; I'm just talking."

"No, come on!"

"Hmm…I mean, we're all different, right? There is no one exactly like you even if you are an identical twin."

"Right, so they say," I agreed.

"And not, because at the same time we all basically want the same things; love, joy, peace, happiness, reasonably good health and something meaningful to do."

"Ok, I'm with you, and?"

"And there are different ways to get there. For me, meditation and the friends I have in my life are essential to it, to me."

"So what IS this thing with meditation?"

I could not quite get what she meant and was beginning to get impatient.

"I'm afraid there is no simple answer to that, at least not any I know of, and it's also beyond mind so-to-speak; you just try it and see what's in there for you. Chances are you might even like it."

"But there must be some meaning to it?" I persisted.

"I once heard Osho say…"

"And who is Osho?"

"Osho was an enlightened Indian man who attracted a lot of people – and still does, although he is no longer in his body…"

"No longer in his body? You mean he's dead?"

"Yes; his body gave up in 1990," Stella replied.

"So…that was even before us. How come you say you have heard him?"

"Because there are hundreds of audios, DVDs, books and transcripts."

"Wow, that's a lot. I'm curious; how did you find him and what is it you were going to say that you had heard him say?"

I was getting confused and she stifled a laugh again.

"I found him – or maybe he found me – when I did a personal growth course. That's when I first tried some of his meditations and heard a few quotes, which all touched and opened something in me that I wouldn't be able to close, even if I wanted to. And I most certainly don't want to. On the contrary, I wanted and want to explore more of it. Since then, I have heard him say a lot of things. Listening to his discourses is one way of meditating for me. He also created other meditation techniques and revived ancient ones. Several of my friends were with him when he was still in his body and are using and spreading these techniques in their work today. And so do I."

"This 'being in the body' and 'leaving the body' is actually a nice way of putting it," I said, realising I had never thought of it that way.

"You think so? Yes, I think so too. It makes it less dramatic, somehow, more like the natural part of life that it is. I heard him say that meditation has no meaning, but it has tremendous significance, or something to that end. That makes it clear, doesn't it?"

I thought that I could get used to that laughter of hers again.

"Clear as mud, thank you."

"Ha, ha, good. You know, we all walk around with wounds from our past that more or less run our lives, usually without us having any clue about it. We're like robots in some sense, programmed to behave one way or another. We all have very good reasons for being the way we are. It helped us survive when we were kids onwards, and it's quite touching what we did and how we developed, doing our best, usually 'unconsciously' or instinctively, in the quest for love, belonging, survival and life. However, I, like many of us, reached a point where I didn't just want to 'survive' anymore. I wanted to live, to feel alive, to enjoy life more. Meditation helps me there and can take me to a space where I can gain awareness of my old patterns – and to put some distance to these old identifications, to create more space and calm inside. It may help me see that today, as the adult I am, I actually have a choice in every situation to act differently to my inner autopilot, if I find it appropriate; if only I am conscious enough

129

to see it, to watch myself and manage that step into a new way of taking action.

"We all have the potential to be the free, responsible individuals we were born to be and not just run around like neurotic robots stuck in the child's programme, haunted by our often quite destructive thoughts. That was long; sorry if I'm lecturing."

"You're not. Now I'm even more curious to hear more and, most likely, with an impatient family waiting at home."

I checked the time, and yes, I was going to be late – again.

"Ok, I'll be brief; for now, anyway. I'd say that we're all like plants or flowers in a way, developed from a seed, and if we find good soil and nourishment we can blossom and even bear fruit. Who knows what kind of flowers we are, or what fruits we might carry. Meditation can bring awareness and inner space, thereby transforming our neuroses into new roses."

"Hmm, you didn't come up with that one now, did you? But ok, it's a nice metaphor and the mud has now been transformed into soil or maybe gravy."

"Let me know when you're hungry for more," Stella laughed.

"I will, Stella, I will."

"Anyway, in my experience, meditation cannot really be explained; it has to be experienced, again and again. In a way, it's like inner exercising or cleansing, and eventually resting. And there's more to it too. Maybe I could compare it to watching a lake; some days there are waves with different intensity and some days it's still and mirror-like. You see something beautiful, so you want more and then you start seeing the beauty of it every day, however the lake is. So you keep watching, or…I don't know."

"Ok, I'll bear that in mind. It was nice talking to you Stella."

"I don't know why you called Carl, but I'm glad you did."

"Mhmm…me too. Actually, it would probably surprise you to hear that I've thought about you quite often and never got in touch, because…because I feel ashamed about how I treated you."

"Oh Carl. Obviously, I wasn't happy when it happened, but you know, it passed, and now is a completely different story, so that shame is really nothing but a waste of energy. Of course you can keep it if you like, but please, not for my sake."

"Thank you…really."

"You're welcome."

There was that almost audible smile again.

"Take care and enjoy the rest of your weekend!"

"Thanks, I will; you too!"

We hung up. That call had taken a turn I never would have expected. Stella also seemed to have taken a turn I never would have expected. Good for her, as it would seem. Making that call turned out to be a very good thing, since somehow it proved to be the beginning of the most valuable friendships I have ever had – the one with Stella and the one with myself.

To this day, I am really thankful that I did not just take the easy way out and send her a friend request on Facebook or Linkedin, or one of those social websites, however useful they may be for networking or for staying connected with distant friends. In fact, we did connect on Linkedin, became friends on Facebook and we even Snapchat sometimes; a part of today's reality.

Chapter 14

Stella Discovers That No Reason Can Be Many Reasons

Being out
I cannot but go in
Again and again
Going in
Taking me no-where
Giving me no-thing
Empty yet full

"According to you, how come this crying mood-mode has been activated in me so much of the time recently?"

If not rhetorical, the question was far-fetched at the least, and I did not really expect an answer from Carl. I mean, how could he possibly know? Especially since I did not. Nevertheless, since it is often easier to see things in others rather than in oneself, I was hoping that Carl might have an answer.

"It is? 'So much of the time recently'– that's an interesting way of putting it."

Carl teased me a little, probably checking if I would go for that kind of bait on a day like this.

"Well...whatever, but yes, it is and I can't really pinpoint why. I mean, why the crying?"

Some people have told me that one of my biggest fears is to show my vulnerability and this resistance to the crying was almost certainly a sign of that.

"Does it matter? Maybe you just need to cry," Carl suggested.

"Yeah, obviously I do."

"Do you really have to have a reason, or two, or three for it? Would you be this impatient if you were laughing instead?"

"Well... no." I had to smile. "And no, apparently I don't, since I don't and do cry."

"How does it feel then? Agonising? Relaxing? Self-pitying?" Carl enquired.

"I don't know; I just feel generally sad lately. It's like I'm consumed by it."

A part of me silently hoped I appeared less helpless than I felt.

"And for no reason?"

"Yes. I mean I can be out walking, or preparing some coffee, or talking to a friend, or just alone not doing anything particular and it overwhelms me. Of course, there are also moments when something affects me; a piece of music, a beautiful morning or sunset, the moon, or some beautiful words, or a loving act...and then there is this different crying." I didn't know how to describe it.

"It all sounds beautiful to me," Carl stated softly.

"In a way, I feel so too, yet I can't help wondering, since this other crying doesn't really feel like it brings any relaxation, or release, or relief; at least not any noticeable effect."

"And you don't want it to be there? Maybe it's because you're kind of fighting it?"

"Oh, I don't mind it."

I could hear the contradiction.

"So that's why you're bringing it up?" Carl could be quite astute.

134

"Well, it is the way it is, and I let it be there, watch it, investigate what might be behind it, hold myself, meditate; and sometimes I guess you could say I escape by watching a film, or doing some surfing on the Internet, or looking in the fridge for something to eat."

"And if you look back at other times when you have felt this crying mood or sadness, what's caused it? Any examples that come to your mind?"

"Often there has been an obvious reason and a feeling of rejection, of not being wanted or good enough, like when boyfriends have broken up with me, or not wanted to enter into a relationship, or when I've not got a job after several interviews."

I noticed that a part of me did not want to go deeper into this, but another part did.

"Sounds like valid reasons for a good cry to me. Anything else?"

"Feeling lonely, like not really belonging anywhere or with anyone, not feeling needed or important; that I come pretty far down on the list of the people I love...and on mine."

"And none of it has been there lately?" Carl probed.

"No, not like that. I mean, you could say that deep down some remainders of those wounds and feelings are always there, and every now and then something triggers them to come to surface and at times I get hooked. But no; I can't really see any such triggers having occurred lately."

I really did not like this feeling of hopelessness. Perhaps that was actually the clue I was looking for; earlier experiences had shown me that the more I was fighting against something, the stronger its grip

135

became. As someone once said; what I give energy to grows and fighting is usually a strong energy.

"So we have crying and sadness happening for no reason...or maybe every reason?"

"Meaning?"

"Well...I don't want to reason away your feeling, but anyone could have their moments, or even periods, of crying and sadness no matter what their situation. As we've said before, it's a part of life and, after all, you do have a number of circumstances that would intrinsically induce the feelings you mention, at least in my world..." Carl hesitated.

"Oh yeah...like what circumstances?"

"All that you mentioned, together with the different bodily challenges you have, with no one in particular to support you on a regular basis. I dare say that most of us want to be in a healthy, functioning body and to have someone special to love and to love us. We also like to feel that we have something meaningful to do, as well as friends, a social network and free time. You have said so yourself."

Carl looked at me a little apprehensively.

"And you're implying that I don't have any of that?"

I looked back at him, a little surprised and hurt.

"No that's not what I'm saying... or...to be honest, maybe it is?" Carl admitted.

"Well, thank you for your honesty; I like that, but I do beg to differ. Ok, it is a fact that the body does what it does and there is only so much I can do about it. And yes, I am single, and sometimes wish that someone was waiting for me somewhere or at home, but usually I feel I have a rich life with friends I love and that I have meaningful things to do."

I was aware that I may have sounded defensive, but to keep ruminating over those things that are no less than facts; well, then sometimes enough really is enough.

"Ok, good, that's great, and you have your moments, of course. Do you also feel like you're living your full potential? Is there something you have not yet found or realised? No hidden corners or regrets?" Carl asked.

"Hmm…that's a good one."

I had to admit there might be something there.

"It is?"

"Yes. Something I kind of stumble on every now and then. Certainly, I sometimes wonder if there is such a thing as a purpose to one's life, to my life and whether I have found it and live it. Perhaps I live it without knowing or realising; that whatever 'I' think, or feel, or do, or want, doesn't mean that much, if anything, in case there is this larger intelligence with a wider perspective. Maybe all I need to do is to relax into my being, where there is nowhere to go, nothing to do; to just be, here now, not being caught by thoughts dragging me back into the past, or throwing me into worries about the future. If I stick to 'now', my problems actually have a tendency to disappear."

"Have you ever experienced that, that absolute 'now' or whatever you like to call it?" Carl probed.

"Umm, yes, I'd say so. I'd say I've had glimpses; I can't really put it into words, but the feeling I've had could be described as 'nothing', an overflowing, fulfilling nothing. It is quite a paradox."

"It sure sounds like it. I remember you mentioning that 'nothing' before."

"Yes, I'm sure I did. It's kind of funny, you know, how there are people with brilliant minds, like Stephen Hawking for instance and beyond all comparison, who seems to be set on finding a theory of everything, while someone like me is set on finding a practice of nothing…or not even a practice; it's more an inner state. In a way, it is far removed from the regular notion of finding and living your full potential, with stating your intention, setting goals and making plans about how to attain them. Or maybe not; maybe that nothingness is our full potential. Who knows? I certainly don't."

"I'm relieved you mentioned Professor Hawking as a non-comparable example. I mean he is one of a kind. Don't ask me where this comes from, but it just struck me that the everything and nothing might very well be closer to one another than we imagine; they might even end up meeting somehow. For the record, I think you know more than you think you do," Carl said reassuringly.

"Ha, ha, really? And yes, he is amazing and inspires me to try to live my life as well and fully as I can, to enjoy what is there, to share what I have and to care for the ones I have. That includes, to some extent, those I don't have." I smiled at him.

"Well, that doesn't sound like a cause for crying." Carl smiled back.

"Ha, ha, no…if not out of gratitude, which also happens. You're right; in many ways I am on my own. At the end of the day, we all are, basically. No one can really live our life for us. I remember once when a friend I love deeply told me that I don't have to carry it all by myself all the time; that I could come to her and that there would probably be other friends too, if I gave them the chance. I was so touched and grateful. Naturally, I started crying. Even now, just remembering and talking about it with you, touches me. Despite knowing this, I sometimes still have a fear of reaching out or allowing myself to receive, although I do long for it."

I could feel my heart pounding and was close to tears. Again.

"So we are alone – and not. No man is an island, you know. Well, maybe we are and, if so, we need bridges to other islands, don't we?" Carl reached out his hand and I took it.

"Yes, fortunately."

Bridges. Over gaps, between islands, between people, between emotions too. Again and again I am reminded how we cannot choose to feel only joy and not sadness. The whole range of emotions and feelings come together and if we cut one off, we cut them all off, since they are all linked together and none is right or wrong as such. The human being and body come with the full package. Luckily. In between, are these glimpses of nothing, where everything somehow just is; like silence, which holds every sound, from the most ear-splitting noise, to the subtlest tones from the strings in a symphony by Beethoven. It all has its place.

Chapter 15

Carl Leaves the Corporate World to Incorporate Staying Open

Voices were speaking
Listening
I heard it all
Yet nothing was said

"So, let's get down to business."

"What?? What business?" Stella looked startled.

"Ha, ha, I had a feeling that would provoke a reaction," I replied, feeling rather pleased.

"Aha, and you got the reaction you wanted?"

"I can't really say what reaction I wanted, to be honest. I suppose I just wanted to see if I could surprise you and where that might lead."

"'Lead'? Like in getting somewhere physically, or like in giving us something unexpected to talk about?" Stella smiled.

"Yes...well, the latter I'd say."

"So let's talk about that," Stella suggested.

"That what?" I obviously did not follow her.

"Yes!" she exclaimed.

"You mean talk about 'yes'?"

"Yes!"

"Ok. What about it?"

I was a little doubtful about her suggestion.

"Well...what would you say?"

"What would I say? I'd say I'm beginning to regret my little move and I'd say it can be a very powerful little word." I was trying to buy some time.

"Now we're getting somewhere."

She seemed to go for something I did not yet see.

"Hold your horses, we haven't really started yet, have we?"

"It sounds to me like you're onto something."

She looked at me with a certain amusement.

"I am?" I looked at her and she nodded, so I continued. "I am. Ok, the power of yes. For instance, when I ask someone for something that I want and get a 'yes', that makes me happy and that's a good feeling, right? So the 'yes' has the power to make me feel good."

"Now, wait a minute. I still feel you're onto something, but now it sounds to me like you've gone off the track a bit," Stella interrupted.

"I have?"

I was happy she had at least thought I had been on track, but now all of a sudden I was off track, without realising it. So much for my experimenting.

"Yeah. When you get the kind of 'yes' you mentioned, are you really putting the power where it belongs?"

"Well, the 'yes' makes me happy and a 'no' wouldn't." I fumbled a bit.

"Yeah, ok, and behind the 'yes' or 'no'…?" Stella pressed.

"There's someone whom I asked for something, and thus gave them the power to make me happy – or not. Ok, got it, I think; for now, anyway."

"That's a pretty good start, isn't it? Even though the power may not lie in the words themselves, but

141

with the one who utters them, the two small words 'yes' and 'no' generally do have very different consequences, which in itself gives a certain power to the one who gets to decide between them."

"Indeed. One makes me happy and the other makes me unhappy," I agreed.

"Well, that would depend on how you put the question, wouldn't it?"

Stella seemed to be at least one step ahead of me.

"Of course. How do you mean?"

We both laughed.

"Don't worry, I get it. I hope. Sometimes it is a 'no' that makes me happy, and not a 'yes', like if I asked someone if the opponents to my favourite football team won the match."

"That and other life-threatening possibilities," Stella added.

"Exactly!"

"Maybe one could say that there actually are certain…intrinsic qualities, let's call them, to those two little words." Now Stella was apparently onto something.

"And that would be?" I enquired.

"What popped up is that 'yes' opens, and 'no' closes. Would you agree?"

"How could I not? But yes, if I say yes to you now, I open to that possibility of possibilities, and if I'd said no, that same road would have been closed."

"I agree."

"And come to think of it, I'd say that many of us are more inclined to one or the other." I knew I was.

"How do you mean?"

"Some people have a tendency to blurt out 'yes' or 'no' automatically in many situations, but maybe it's with certain people. However, I often hear myself say 'no' to a suggestion without having given it too much consideration, if any at all. I can't say that I like that 'automatic no', because more than once I would like to have bitten off my tongue, or at least remained silent," I confessed.

"Why?"

"Because I feel so negative and non-encouraging." I shook my head.

"And that's not how you would want to be, or be perceived?"

"Right, not in general. But sometimes I do try to rewind the tape so-to-speak, to give the suggestion some consideration and at times say, 'Hey, my no was a bit quick' or something and come up with a yes instead."

"Well, that's already a big step, isn't it?" Stella leaned back in the sofa.

"Yes, I guess it is."

"So we could say that 'yes' and 'no' in some sense could be an inner attitude, couldn't we? And again, it becomes pretty obvious that all these automatic programmes and behaviours that we seem to run are less than…maybe appropriate is the word?" Stella reflected.

"I think so too. I can also see it the other way around, not least with the kids."

"Aha? How?"

"With them, I have a tendency to say yes all the time when they want something in the material sense, which becomes quite obvious, for example, at birthdays and Christmas, when I see to it that the majority of their wishes for presents are fulfilled – with the help of their grandparents and my sister, of course.

Most likely, they will end up spoiled, thinking they can always have what they want." I shook my head. "I'd better see to it that we bring some more awareness there too."

"That's probably worth a try. I don't know if you feel this is the case, but could it be that if they get 'everything', then the chances are they will become blasé and won't really appreciate, or enjoy any of it that much. It becomes almost overwhelming, or...?" Stella had a point.

"Yes, and the thing is, we create it. I remember when they were smaller and were still occupied with a present they had opened – usually the first one containing a toy they liked. They would have been satisfied with that one for a good while, but then we encouraged them to stop playing and open the next one. It also happens the other way around too, when I often say no when they want me to play with them. Generally, I'm just busy with the phone with the excuse of having to check something; not out of necessity, but out of habit. I mean, when I think about it..." I shook my head.

"It makes you think again maybe?" Stella smiled.

"Hopefully."

I took a moment to look out the window and sighed, making an inner decision to really try to be more aware and change these patterns.

"One other aspect of this, the yes and no, and always saying yes, is that if you can't say no, then your yes seems to lose some of its value." She kept us on track.

"Hmm...you mean that you get taken for granted, and in some sense not really appreciated; similar to the story about the two brothers, or rather, the two sons?"

"You mean the one about the prodigal son? Where there was one who went on his adventures, while the other loyally stayed at the farm, and when the travelling one came back, he was the one who was appreciated by the father?" Stella asked.

"That very one," I confirmed.

"Yeah, I also think that story taps into it quite well. I have to admit that when I first heard it, I thought it was pretty unfair."

Stella looked as though she had recalled some memories, but it didn't feel like an appropriate moment to ask. I knew that she used to be the loyal type.

"Uhum, me too, although in a way I can see the point. He goes off to see the world and makes the choice to come back – for whatever reason."

"Exactly – for whatever reason, and the other had stayed on, for whatever reason. Would you say the reason matters? What if coming back was his last lifeline and he had to, because he couldn't make it otherwise? Or maybe he realised what a fantastic place it was and chose it out of appreciation rather than duty? Maybe the one who stayed on had done so simply because he wasn't up to anything else? Perhaps if we knew the story better we'd have better ideas. Anyway, 'yes' and 'no', which might appear so clear, actually have implications, which I'd say may make it not so clear," Stella continued.

"By that, you mean to say?"

"Well, if you say yes to something, that also means that you say no to something else and vice versa."

"Yes, indeed. Are we making things complicated, or what?" I could not help it, and we both laughed.

"Maybe it's best to ask our minds to rest a bit and stick to our gut feelings." She put her hands on her belly.

"If we can feel it."

"Yes, that can be a bit tricky in the beginning, then trusting it will be the next challenge, I'd say. It might take some practice and getting used to."

"It most likely will. So, getting back to business, today's conclusion about yes and no would be?" I felt it was time to round this subject up.

"Oh la, la! How about staying present in the moment and the situation at hand, and give it a few seconds before you speak?" She smiled.

"Ha, ha, yes, that would already mean huge progress; at least in my case."

"Not only in yours, I'd say, but in mine too."

I have often noticed that in business and corporate meetings, a lot of words are spoken, yet not much is actually being said, despite the huge salaries that some are paid. This afternoon with Stella also contained quite a lot of spoken words and no agenda to be followed. Nevertheless, I had the feeling that something actually had been said. I would even call it something useful, like that one-line conclusion Stella came up with; the three or so seconds. Evidently easy, but still so difficult to incorporate into everyday life. As I was told in military service, we might lose a battle and still win the war. That is an awful metaphor – at least in this case. How about, 'in order to have crops to harvest, we must sow seeds'? Yes, that feels much better.

Chapter 16

Stella Playfully Reveals Her Passions

Cells vibrating
Pulsating presence
Aliveness acting
In tune with all
Beyond time
Beyond ideas
Nothing else matters
All there is, is

"Carl, did I tell you about that talk I had with my niece Ellika?"

"No, I don't think so. I mean, I don't know; what are you referring to?"

"…When she asked me about passion and I told her about one of my little adventures, among other things."

I sometimes wish I would learn to keep my mouth shut.

"No, I don't think I've heard about that one. Why?" Carl seemed intrigued.

"I'm a bit concerned about her using it as an excuse for doing something stupid one day. I can only imagine what her parents would say, and you're a parent."

"Come on; it can't be that bad. Or can it? And she's a sensible young woman who loves you, isn't she?" Carl reassured.

"Yeah, well, she is, and sensitive."

"So tell me; if nothing else, at least you've captured my interest!"

"I have? Well...ok; just to have your parental opinion. We were having one of those shopping days, eating out and so on together, and while waiting for the food in a restaurant, all of a sudden she exclaimed: 'Passion! I want passion!' I looked at her, a little surprised by the turn of the conversation. She looked back at me and continued: 'Did you ever play around, or go for your passion? I mean...you don't have to answer if you don't want to.'

"I said to her, 'Well... you know...actually I have, a couple of times, when the energy was there. There was one time especially when there was really strong passion; passion out of sexual attraction, I mean, since I understand that's what you're referring to. She said, 'Ha, ha, yes, come on, now you have to tell me more!' I said that I didn't know whether it was that interesting, but Ellika was keen to know, so I told her.

"I was on a business trip when it happened. I remember the butterflies in my belly. 'God, why is he such a gentleman? Or, thank goodness he is such a gentleman.' Thoughts, feelings, attraction, desire were all on high gear. I noticed him the first morning in a welcoming reception and apparently he noticed me too. Tall, slim, well-toned, sun-kissed and handsome in rugged way. To me, he really had that 'something'. At lunch, he saw to it that we were introduced to each other and exchanged business cards. By accident, I dropped his card on the floor and he was ever so quick to pick it up and make sure I had it; quite cute. The mingling in the afternoon was quite pleasant for once. Even exciting actually."

148

"You never told me about this!" Carl looked at me and smiled.

"Well, you know, there's a first time for everything."

"So there is, and?"

"The rest is history." In vain, I attempted to cut it short.

"No reason not to continue then, please."

"Ok. You asked for it," I muttered.

"Apparently the attraction was mutual, because a colleague made some comments, which took me by surprise. Eventually, he asked about my plans for the evening and suggested I come with him. Spending the evening with him and his friends was like a no-choice choice; my boss and colleagues were suddenly not important at all. So you could say I went for some networking. Late that evening, he insisted on walking with me back to my hotel to make sure I returned safely. Without any hints, we stopped by the entrance where we talked for a while before he said he'd go back, and leaned down for a kiss. Then he smiled, stroked my cheek, turned his back and walked away. And there I was, not knowing whether I should be satisfied with the fact that he did everything right, or run after him. I really was in two minds, as if one wouldn't be enough. I settled with the first alternative. My pulse was quite high, my cheeks were warm and my body was almost shivering. 'Damn!' I thought. 'How could I let him go?'"

"A gentleman, of course. No wonder you had some expectations of me."

"Oh, well, I assure you, nothing that I didn't think you'd be up to." I looked at him and smiled before I went on.

"The next morning, he arrived a little late to the same session that I was attending, without our having agreed on anything. Our eyes met, he sat down next to me, and I don't think either of us could concentrate on the presentations. My heart was pounding and our feet sometimes touched slightly, causing a rush of energy through my whole body. The following session was his presentation and I was, of course, in the audience. He did well – and I was proud of him, which I told myself was silly and ridiculous, since we had only met some 24 hours earlier. At lunch, after the obligatory handshaking, introductions, and brief discussions, we managed to go shopping, just to get away for a moment or two. After all, the venue was situated close to a mall. In one of the shops, he touched my back lightly with his hand as he passed me to try a jacket on. It felt like an electric shock. In the afternoon there was no return. Luckily my hotel was just across the street.

"'Finally on our own!' he said. I could only agree. For a moment though, a voice inside of me tried to tell me that it was too much of a cliché and what good could come out of it? Another voice made it clear that this was the 1990s, not the 1890s, and I should go for it. So I did. We put the action on hold somewhat, since some precautions were needed, but that didn't hinder the exploring of each other and rather increased the excitement. I was so happy that, for some strange reason, I had bought some nice new lingerie before going."

"You really think he – or maybe I should say we – care about lingerie at a moment like that?" Carl joked.

"Yes, I do. You mean you don't?"

"Probably not often, no. I mean, it's mainly there to be taken off, but you know, there's always the exception to the rule."

"Ha, ha, well, anyway, whatever, at least it made me feel better."

"Ok, that's fair enough. I'm beginning to feel like some kind of audio-voyeur here. So?"

"Neither of us felt that we could elope from the formal dinner that night and, despite the fact that he was a little late, he still managed to get a seat at the table where I was sitting. Later, when someone had to leave early, he sat next to me. I'm sure the food was good and the speeches eloquent, but we couldn't get out of there soon enough.

"That man sure knew his way with me. Lying there next to him, there was a moment when I looked at him and said, 'If I died right now, I'd die a very happy woman.' He looked at me, smiled and replied, 'Hopefully, you're just going to die a little, like the French say, but again and again.'

"A little later, he commented, 'God, we literally couldn't live further apart!' and 'We have to see each other again soon!' We were both wondering what had hit us. He was married, although supposedly divorcing, so we would inevitably find an opportunity."

"You know; we men can be so convincing," Carl laughed.

"Yes, you can, and I really didn't think I had any reason to doubt him."

"And you can be so innocent."

"Hmm, yes I can, and fortunately, I'd say. It balances the cynicism and irony that I'm afraid is more easily accessible to me."

151

"You're right; innocence is often a very beautiful quality – but I'm not totally convinced you're right about your cynicism. Anyway, and then what? Let's not change the subject." Carl eagerly kept me on track.

"Well, you can imagine how much I hated saying goodbye to him. I had planned a couple of weeks of travelling around, enjoying some sun and beaches, and all I wanted was just to go back home, save my vacation days, and plan our next meeting. Upon my return in the office, I had emails from him waiting for me! Our emailing was pretty intense for the following months, painting all kinds of scenarios and occasions to the best of our imagination. For various reasons, our next meeting did not happen until years later. And as beautiful a little adventure as it was, it was apparently not supposed to be anything else. I'm very grateful for having had that with him. I wouldn't like to be without it."

"I bet. Now I'm a bit jealous too. So how did Ellika react when you told her?"

"She looked a bit perplexed and said something like, 'Wow! Thank you. I don't know what to say. So no regrets then?' And I remember answering, 'No! What I did sometimes regret was that I wasn't more wild and crazy and put myself on a flight there and then and just showed up. He did say he had wished for that, too, but neither of us did actually do it.' Then she commented, 'So the old saying is right then? You might regret some stupid things you have done, but the things you regret most are the stupid things you haven't done.'"

"And now dear Auntie, how did you reply to that?" Carl asked teasingly.

"Oh, I said something like, 'Maybe it has a point sometimes. So, what is it you want to do? I wouldn't want to have your parents on my neck for having encouraged you to do something reckless.' And she tried to reassure me by saying, 'Don't worry. I wouldn't do anything you wouldn't do.' I looked at Ellika and laughed, saying, 'And by that you mean to reassure me? Now, tell me or do I have to use force?' I smiled at her and we went on with our dinner and talk a while longer."

"Well, it sounds to me like you don't have to worry too much about your influence on her," Carl tried to convince me.

"Thank you. I just hope you're right. Teenage girls, and probably boys too, have a lot of dreams and wishes and so does my niece. I admit that her question made me reflect some more that evening."

"Oh yeah, walking down memory lane thinking about that guy?"

"Maybe a little, but more about passion," I emphasised, while feeling my cheeks burning.

"Uhum, well, it sounded like you had a great experience together."

"Ha, ha, you really are jealous, aren't you?"

"Come on, don't tease me; I already told you." Carl blushed too.

"You're sweet. Actually, it was more about passion as such, in general. I mean, if anything, I have come to experience passion in many more ways than just sex and intimate relationships; passion for life, meditation, friends, work, music, food. Would that be something 'people' would accept? Would that be something I'd tell a man? Maybe not on a first or second date, at least not with those words, but he would probably still discover that I am a passionate and playful woman."

"Why not? But I think you're right; you'd probably want to save those passions for later – or play with it – and he would eventually discover and appreciate how passionate you are. If not, that would be his loss."

"Ha, ha, like I said, you're sweet...and sexy..."

"Finally!"

I enjoyed the lightness that we usually ended up with, no matter how serious or heavy the themes of our talks at first appear. Some playfulness and humour do make life easier, and definitely more fun, so why take it as seriously as many of us often do? In my experience, the seriousness often has a tendency to happen by itself anyway, without our having to impose it. Like the old saying that laughter prolongs your life. Be that as it may, it certainly makes it more enjoyable.

Chapter 17

Carl Brings Up the Meaning of Life and Comes Down with Himself

Why? Where to? How? When?
Spending your life and then?
Is there something like a goal?
To find blessing for the soul?
So many questions we could ask
Not seeking answers, is that our task?

"What would you say; do you think there's a meaning to life?"

I had a feeling this could take us anywhere, which was part of the enjoyment of our talks.

"Ok, so big questions today, huh?" Stella switched off her phone or at least activated flight mode and put it in her bag.

"Big, or maybe very small; that's another Question."

"I don't know what to say, or rather, where to start, but let's say it depends."

"Depends? Depends on what?"

I almost felt an aggression build up in me that I could not explain. I wondered where that was coming from. Was it a feeling of not being respected, or of being belittled? It would probably be helpful for me to have a round with myself on this one. Stella looked at me and I thought I could see curiosity and amusement in her expression.

155

"I'd say it depends on where I am at, Carl. Not the meaning of life as such, but what I think. Sometimes when I've been low, I haven't seen any point to anything, let alone this silly life, which could always end at any moment. I mean, you run the rat race, often work like crazy and, if you're lucky, you have a healthy body, make good money, try to eat and drink reasonably well, get enough exercise, fall in love with someone and have kids. Then the fighting starts or get worse and sooner or later, 'boom', you're gone." Stella shrugged, and smiled.

"Well, biologically at least, some would argue that having children is the purpose of life." I was, after all, the father of two.

"So, you mean the only reason we're born is to procreate?" Stella asked, somewhat appalled.

"I didn't say that was my view; I just said that some would maybe argue so. Well, anyway, what about all the people who, for various reasons, don't or can't have children? People like you for instance?" I looked at her, probably with a level of trepidation.

"Ha, ha, exactly. What the fuck am I doing here? One of God's mistakes. What about me; what about us? What right do we have if we don't 'contribute' by having children?"

By the way in which she spoke, I could feel she was not as offended or aggrieved as the words might imply, but rather pretending for the sake of it, or to add some more colour to the discussion.

"How much do I get if I give you an answer to that? Millions in the bank and a happy life ever after, or?"

It would seem like Stella had dealt with this issue before.

"You wish!" I smiled.

"Yeah, maybe I do and wish I had an answer, but in some sense you do have a point. I mean, more than once I have been told that children are the meaning of life, but since I don't have any, I can't really understand this or that. Maybe that's right; who knows? Anyway, one conclusion then would be: no kids, no purpose, but that is also putting a hell of a lot of responsibility on the kids that they don't deserve. Talk about living through the children. The question remains. After all, many of us keep asking ourselves and each other – children or not – what the meaning of life is. I guess we could agree on at least one thing..." She paused.

"And that would be?" I asked.

"That there is no one, intrinsic, general, apparent meaning. That we all have to find out for ourselves what gives meaning to our own lives and do what we can to live accordingly, if we want to and like to. Or maybe find a way to accept the 'fact' that there is no purpose and just enjoy living this wondrous mystery, moment by moment, letting the path be the goal and thereby the meaning."

She had some water and looked as though she was enjoying it almost as much as I have seen her enjoy her coffee or chocolate.

"Enjoying the present of the present, you mean?"

"Bingo, Sir!" She pointed to me and we both laughed.

"I must, however, say that children really do give a sense of purpose though," I reasoned.

"I'm sure, and I wouldn't wish that to be otherwise. As long as we don't make them the only meaning."

157

"No, you have a point there. And unfortunately, far too often, children end up in situations similar to that, it would seem."

I thought of all the children I knew who, according to my perception, were made the only focus of one or both of the parents, usually when the parents' relationship was not working so well.

"Yes, I'm afraid you're right. It's probably quite common for people to have children because it's 'part of the package'; what one 'should' have. Maybe the relationship is in need of a boost, or some kind of metaphorical glue, or life feels pretty boring or meaningless without children, or we feel lonely and long to be needed, and then of course there is biology." Stella shrugged her shoulders again.

"Not to be forgotten; even animals have kids. And what are we but animals with an intellect, like some people have described us?" I added.

"That makes us a bit different to animals, but which is sometimes good to have, yet at other times has a tendency to create problems for us, both as individuals and as a collective," Stella argued.

"Indeed. We are also social beings, who want and need to feel that we belong somewhere, and preferably to several 'groups', like family, friends, job, society..."

I could have added social clubs, brotherhoods and more to the list.

"And even if many of us are quite used to the feeling of being an outsider, the bottom line is that I think we would all like to feel like a part rather than apart." She looked around, then back at me.

"We do, with the odd exception to the rule. I mean, there are, of course, situations where people who can be a bit... rebellious, let's say, are highly needed.

158

Looking at history, it's obvious that we can do the most horrible things in order to belong. I'm afraid we can see that in many awful things that happen these days too."

I held up the weekly magazine I had bought on the way. I still enjoy the paper editions sometimes, even though e-magazines on the iPad or tablet have their advantages too.

"We can, and the situations moving towards the extremes are usually not very pleasant." Stella shook her head in despair.

"No, so for now let's stay with our more everyday kind of situations. You know, the only person you can change is yourself." I pointed at her.

"Ha, ha, yes, and if you want to change the world, start with yourself, right?" She pointed back at me.

"Ha, ha, yes; I had that one coming."

Our hands met in a high-five.

It's a question that many of us seem to come back to again and again, like stubborn two-year-olds, since we somewhere know this is a question that cannot really be answered. But we can explore – explore what gives meaning, purpose and joy to our days; how and with what we want to fill them. It is up to each and every one of us. No quick fix like a pill to take, a book to read, a manual to follow, a course to attend, a thing to buy, or an expert to ask. What a bummer.

Or instead – what a relief. There seems to be at least one clue. It is not about the things we buy or have, or else the richest people would also be the happiest, which does not appear to be the case; that kind of satisfaction seems to wane quickly. It seems to be more about what we do and with whom; activities that give joy and wellbeing to our body and soul, like seeing friends and people we like and love, sharing experiences, walking in nature, singing in a choir or hugging.

So, I'd better start with and in myself. Here now, the point of no return – or, the point of returning to myself.

Chapter 18

Stella's Anger Management Leads the Way

Carrying my rage
I could not be sage
Acknowledging a feeling
Standing my ground
Like losing burden not kneeling
Relaxation was found

"You know, for a long time I believed I hardly ever got angry." I had a soft spot for the subject of anger.

"Well, you didn't, did you? As far as I remember from the years when we were together, I could probably have counted on one hand the number of times you got angry." Carl looked first at his hands, then at me.

"That's probably true, but now I can see that I did. I just didn't feel it or recognise it. I would say I had learnt to repress it pretty well."

"Is that so bad?" Carl was obviously a bit perplexed.

"Not if you listen to the underlying rules and conditions in our society, and in most of our families. You know, like those old sermons and values instilled into us by the church, politicians, teachers and our parents, but once you start listening to your body and what's going on inside, it is probably not very healthy."

"You're not saying we should give into and express every anger impulse we have, do you? I mean that could be rather terrible," Carl said, disapprovingly.

"No, that's not what I'm saying. Let's say that I've discovered the importance of acknowledging it, first of all to myself; to feel it, deal with it internally and ultimately express it in a responsible way and not by verbally, physically or in any other way attacking the other person. Instead, we should use it as an energy and strength in, hopefully, a creative and constructive way."

I knew this might sound easier than it actually is for most of us.

"Sounds good, but I still don't quite get it," Carl admitted.

"Ok. Do you remember a time when you got really mad or pissed off?" I asked.

"Sure."

"How did that feel?"

"I felt like exploding, and in a way I did, getting all hot, shouting all kinds of mean things that I regretted afterwards." Carl appeared remorseful.

"Exactly! That's usually – or at least often – what happens. Someone or something triggers us, or rather the built-up repressed anger in us, and we react disproportionately, maybe even aggressively. There's usually a hell of a lot of energy in it."

"Oh yes!" Carl agreed.

"And how much energy do you think it takes to control and suppress all that energy?"

"Even more."

"Exactly. And what effect can we suspect that suppression has on us?"

"Feeling uptight, tired, tense, not very alive. I'm beginning to see what you're getting at. Look around; no wonder most of them – us – look rather dull, or feel like walking time bombs."

Carl pointed with his head to the others in the room, with some new energy awakening in him, as it seemed.

"Yeah." I had thought the same thing. "Most of us, if not all, have a killer inside. You have no idea how many times I've killed a number of people. Actually you included."

"Really? I feel quite alive though."

"I'm happy you do – I wouldn't want it any other way and that is one of the many benefits of one of the active meditations I sometimes do, called Osho Dynamic Meditation."

"So you mean we should acknowledge the anger and learn to contain it until we can express it in some kind of appropriate and civilised way, like running, hitting a punch bag, screaming in the forest, or a car – parked of course – or whatever?" Carl now even had more energy in his voice.

"Something to that end."

"Why on Earth don't they teach that in school?"

"Maybe because anger is a forbidden and fearful feeling from very early on, since the way we learn to deal with it – or rather, not deal with it – is so often connected to aggression and maybe even violence. This is what happens when we repress it, but none of us realise that there is an upside to it too. I mean, I'm not advocating walking around as an angry bird; it's just that anger, or rather that energy, and owning it, seems to hold what we would need to distance ourselves from situations that no longer are good for us. And maybe having access to that energy would also make us something other than obedient marionettes putting duty before everything else."

I tried to illustrate by imitating a marionette with some little movements.

"Yeah, we probably wouldn't be so docile and eager to fit in, since our inner strength most likely would be, if not tangible, at least feel-able – and usable."

"I cannot help but thinking that in the long run it would be a gain for all of us, also as a collective, since we most certainly would be more relaxed and creative. Maybe we would do our own thing more easily, that which we enjoy and are good at, instead of what is expected of us. That would almost certainly increase health, joy and productivity."

"Indeed. Did you ever think about going into politics?" Carl jested.

"Ha, ha, goodness no; I'm quite happy solving the world's problems over a cup of coffee in good company."

"Although I do enjoy it your way, I dare say it is perhaps a pity."

"Ha, ha, enough for today. So what are your plans for the weekend?"

I thought he might have had something in mind, since we had a long weekend coming up.

"You mean besides having a good screaming run in the forest, which just got added to the list?"

"Yes."

"Well, we have some work to do in the garden, then some friends will be over for dinner on Saturday. And you?"

164

"Nice. I'll probably be off to the cottage and have a few late mornings."

"Let's hope this beautiful weather will last." Carl crossed his fingers.

"Yes, that would be great." I looked out and had a glimpse of the moonlight. "By the way, how could I forget; did you see it?"

"Did I see what?"

"The moon! The light!"

"Now? When?"

"On the way here! You didn't see it? What a pity! I was so lucky driving here apparently at the right moment. I wish I'd had my camera. I didn't think of my phone, but it wouldn't have done justice to the real thing and, anyway, I was driving. It was just so beautiful that it almost made me cry. The road turned a little and there it was, the full moon just above the tree tops, in this kind of cold, steely blue, but not quite dark sky. It was so much bigger than yesterday and with an almost warm light. It was just so beautiful!"

It was one of those moments when I was simply struck by the beauty around us.

"Wow, I wish I had seen it."

"Yeah, I wish you had too. Imagine the sky just after sunset; the colours, the horizon, a dark grey lake and the silhouette of the forests and hills contrasting against the sky. Amazing! That incredibly intense glowing orange, merging into a soft, bright pink, fading into a light, almost transparent blue and then blending into a darker blue. It was simply breath-taking!" I wished I could paint.

"I think I almost can see it before me; all the beauty nature provides is really amazing. No matter how we humans may try to duplicate it, we're just not

165

there. Nature is, without exception I dare say, always more beautiful." Carl made his point.

"Yes, how could something that existence, nature created, create something more beautiful than its creator did and keeps on doing?" I smiled.

"Some people have almost made it though, if you ask me."

"Like?"

"Well, take Michelangelo's Pietà or David for example. He's more beautiful than any man, I'd say."

Carl did pick a glorious example.

"To the eye, yes, he is extremely well-proportioned, fit, handsome…and big. He's perfect – and stone-dead; although a stunning, extraordinary piece of art and craft."

I remembered the first time I saw the original in Galleria dell'Accademia in Florence, and was moved to tears, even though I had seen the copy outside Palazzo Vecchio many times.

"Hmm, well yes, that's something to take into consideration. We seem to want living beauty, don't we?" Carl looked content.

"Well, I do anyway. And as much as we think we want and strive for something or someone perfect, I have a feeling that we'd soon discover that perfect is dead. If we want aliveness, life, we'd better accept that together with that comes change, then change again. Thereby, our perfect ideal just cannot last and so we have imperfection, which in many ways has its own perfection and beauty."

I was thinking of all the times I had been wearing certain clothes or had my hair done for a certain occasion, but as soon as I sat down, the clothes would be wrinkled, and as soon as I went outside, the wind would blow my hair in all directions, or I would start sweating out of sheer nervousness about not spoiling my outfit. Phew!

"Yeah, when you think of it, looking at interior design or fashion magazines, even so-called perfectly styled rooms, or models for that matter, don't feel very alive. They are more like museums or dolls; examples of the current trends of course, but usually boring. I've sometimes asked myself why it becomes boring and now I understand that it's probably because everything is too much in place, fixed, perfect, dead." Carl snapped with his fingers.

"I think so too." I couldn't disagree.

"It's wonderful to see the beauty around us, maybe where we don't expect it, or when and where it's not according to any given aesthetic rule, like you just described the moon and the light." Carl gazed at me and moved his head, as if he wanted to see me in different ways and angles. "And on top of it, what we find beautiful is in general quite subjective."

"Yes. And coming back to the beautiful moon and light, I'd say that when we do start paying attention, we're actually surrounded by beauty, and not only in nature. For example, I can be moved to tears by music, by a connection to someone, by a caring gesture – even between people I don't know, by the leaves dancing in the wind. Ok, there we go, back to nature again." I smiled.

"Why not, when it is presenting us with such abundance. As you know, beauty, like everything else, lies in the eyes of the beholder." Carl smiled back at me.

"Yes. Sometimes it's the simple things if you open your eyes. I remember, for example, one of those rainy summer days when there was this yearly market and homecoming day with various events in the little village where the cottage is. I was standing there under my umbrella, waiting for the rain to ease off a bit, looking at some elderly ladies in a marquee, making sandwiches and coffee for sale, while some violinists were standing in a corner trying to play, despite the humidity. I was so touched by their dedication and cheerfulness, and...I don't know, maybe community in the original sense is the word I'm looking for."

"Yes, also like when a child comes and wants to sit in your lap or hold your hand." Subconsciously, Carl let his both hands join together.

"And holding hands with a friend, or really meeting the eyes of someone, maybe especially someone you love. It's almost like when talking about all this, I get an urge to bow down in some kind of reverence to existence, to you, even to myself, to us as human beings – who sometimes feel that life is a struggle – and also sometimes just stand in awe before the miracle of life, of love." Saying this, I did not feel particularly nostalgic; it was more in recognition of a fact.

"We're getting quite solemn here, but it has a good taste right now, so why not? And seeing and feeling all this makes me feel so lucky and rich somehow."

"I bet many people, even the wealthy, have not experienced this sense of gratitude and appreciation for 'nothing', or all these 'things' that money can't buy – or for all the expensive goods that they buy without giving it too much of a thought."

"Yeah, just look at all those over-paid managers or sportsmen for example, who can't be satisfied with having say one, two or even three luxurious cars, but have to have 19, like some of them do. It's crazy," Carl sighed.

"Yes, it's almost strange how we seem to function. I remember when I visited some friends who live in a place with the most breathtaking, beautiful view. One of their close neighbours owned several estates, yet he constantly had the shutters closed. Not only did he not let the sun and daylight in, but he was unable to see and enjoy the magnificent view."

I admit that I had thought it was a waste that he lived there; that if I would get the chance I would have the shutters open as much as possible.

"Now I feel even more lucky, thank you."

"Good! I can also see how a part of me is longing to find a way to share this gratitude, to find a way to contribute."

"Yes, that would be wonderful; me too. Any ideas?"

"Oh, I wish, but no doubt we could all start where we are, with the small things, with friendliness and trying to leave this place, this world, a little more beautiful than we found it."

"Yes, indeed."

Anger somehow seems to be a key, or rather the energy used up in suppressed anger; an energy that can become pure strength and vivacity, if we learn to access it, own it, and use it instead of internalising it, or projecting it onto someone else. Do something creative, feel good, relax, see and appreciate the beauty. The more I think about it, the more it astonishes me that we have got such a twisted message about it, when it could be such an asset.

169

For now, I will settle with the challenge to own and use mine and see what might come along with that.

Chapter 19

Carl Touches a World Wide Web

My mind may be busy
And still cannot know
My eyes may be open
And still will not see
My hands may be searching
And still will not find
What I think, and look, and grab for
Seems out of reach for me
Yet what I cannot reach for
Is silently within, and clear, and free
Always available
Everywhere and naught
So the mind may relax
The eyes may be closed
The hands may rest
Settling into being

"You really look like you're enjoying that cappuccino." And I enjoyed watching Stella sipping it.

"Mmmm…probably because I am."

"I don't know if I would say it looks like your first or last."

"Well Carl, as you know it's not my first – or to be more precise, for today it is. Hopefully it's not my last either, but for now my only."

Stella held the cup in front of her with her two hands, and reluctantly put it down.

"Good point!"

"Thank you for bringing it up." Stella looked inquiringly at me.

"My pleasure."

"By the way, may I ask you something?"

"You already did." I laughed. "But sure, go ahead. Please don't expect too much from the answer though, depending on what you're going to ask of course."

"I'll try not to. It's funny that you bring up expectations, since that really touches what I want to ask you." Stella took another sip.

"I guess I could feel it in the air." We both laughed. "And the question still seems to be hanging there, in the air, I mean."

"Would you say that you basically expect things to change, or to remain the same?" Stella asked.

"Things?"

"Well, in general, things, for want of a better word."

"Ok; do I expect things to change or remain the same? Well, thank you for asking."

"My pleasure this time." She smiled.

"I'm trying to buy some time here." I was searching my mind for an opening thought.

"Take your time; we're not in a hurry as far as I know."

"No, we're not, which alas also means that I cannot excuse myself to rush to a very important meeting," I chuckled.

"Ha, ha, you're already there...at that very important meeting I mean," she teased.

I looked at her, perhaps a little more attentively than usual, and she could obviously feel it.

"What?" Stella asked.

"You're right. This is a very important meeting."

We both smiled at each other.

"And you're still buying time, as it would seem."

"I guess I am… and actually I'm afraid you could call me an arrogant bastard."

"Maybe some would say that that's no news," she replied drolly.

"Really?? Ha, ha, right; the last one to notice is most often oneself."

"Usually, yes, but why would you call yourself an arrogant bastard now, unless you were joking?"

"Are you kidding me? That's probably the most serious thing I've said all day!"

"It's still relatively early, but please, continue." Stella played along and encouraged me.

"I said you could call me an arrogant bastard because I just realised that I usually expect things to remain the same, unless I want them to change, and hence if possible change them, or have them changed the way I want. Far too often, I only realise afterwards that there might be changes also that I didn't anticipate, or want. I do something here, and something happens there, which could have done with some further consideration. When you look at it like this, it could be called pretty arrogant, couldn't it? It even sounds a bit grandiose. By the way, you can call me Bruce…the guy who learned that it isn't all that easy to be God and almighty; not that I have been in that position though, luckily."

I made the victory sign, as I related to the movie with Jim Carrey as Bruce Almighty, with whom I felt a certain kinship, and the thought came to me that we really do live in a world wide web, where everything and all is connected in some way beyond our imagination.

"Are you blushing?" Stella laughed and, sensing the warmth in my cheeks, I had to admit that I was. She continued.

"And I agree, it is, and it does to my ears too, but I also think that that is what most of us usually tend to do, without realising it, or even giving it a thought, so welcome to the club."

"And how come you did? Give it a thought, I mean, and ask me this question?" As usual, I was curious.

"I don't know really...or maybe in a way I do. I mean, we all know that we are going to die, that for most people this will happen in what we call an old age, and at 75 we will not have the body of a 25-year-old. Intellectually, we know this, but we still don't really get it; that the fact is that it really will happen to everybody, sooner or later. It is as if we believe we are the exception to the rule. You know, having a body that step-by-step loses some of its functions at a relatively young age is like a reminder, and helps me to become a little bit more aware of different things, like change and status quo. But I probably brought it up right now because of a cold I had the other week; as trivial and banal as that."

"And?" I wanted her to go on.

"Well, as usually happens when you have a cold, I lost the ability to smell and sense tastes. Only this time I guess it felt different to other times, and the thought and following fear of this becoming a permanent state struck me. Then I thought that even though my sense of taste has been affected already, I had still fallen into the trap of taking that status quo for granted."

"But that is very human, isn't it? I mean, wouldn't we somehow overwhelm ourselves if we were constantly aware of and appreciated everything, every little process in the body, in nature and more or less everything all around us?"

I almost got tired just thinking about it and I could see Stella taking a deep breath.

"You're probably right, but still, if for now we stick to the body, I do think that at least a little more awareness of all the body's miraculous functions and what we all get from it, would make us all more loving both to ourselves and others and would make us more present. In short, happier and more content."

"Now you are probably right…so why aren't we?"

"This is turning into 'the hen or the egg' discussion, isn't it?" Stella smiled and continued. "Your guess is as good as mine, but I presume this kind of normal state of taking it for granted is most likely the basis; then the overwhelm-protection you mentioned and our being so focused on the outer, like on achievements, material things, image, not being here now, but in our minds, which is usually in the past or in the future, all play a part."

"And usually we take the body and all what it is doing for us for granted until something happens, like if we get sick or have an accident."

"Exactly, and sometimes we get smaller wake up-calls, you know, like a blister, or a cold, for instance."

"Which suddenly makes you realise how much easier and better life is when that blister is not there." I could easily identify with this one.

"So, here we are in all our grandiosity, wanting to believe we're in control of our lives, that we can plan and have things the way we like it and, oops, a blister

175

can be enough to throw us off our high horses." Stella wiggled her head the way she sometimes does.

"Do you want another cappuccino?" I made a symbolic effort to try to change the subject.

"Ha, ha, no thank you, but I'll have a glass of water, please."

"I'll have one too. Speaking of tastes, it's pretty amazing, isn't it, that water tastes of nothing and yet it is still so good? There's just nothing better when you're thirsty."

"I couldn't agree more."

I went to get our water, noticing that the concept of change kept working in my mind and remembering that many wise people have pointed out the paradox of change being perhaps the only constant thing. And how we often think we are all for change, but then when it happens, we find ourselves resisting or maybe even fighting it – especially if we did not get our own way. How easy it is to get used to whatever we have and, not knowing what we might get, we have a tendency to cling to it, good or bad. We might manage to change one thing, somewhat naively assuming and expecting that what we do not want to change will stay the same; some kind of wishful thinking of the theoretical 'ceteris paribus' put into practice, not realising that in reality everything is linked together and we cannot really isolate and change just one thing without it affecting everything else around us.

On my way back, I realised that it takes strength and courage, not to mention flexibility and openness, to surrender to change, and that our resistance might have its roots in our inherent fear of the unknown, since there we are vulnerable and do not yet know what we will have to face and cope with in the future. Still, there is also excitement, which is sometimes stronger than fear – and what makes us move forward, explore, experience and grow. All this on one of these ordinary weekdays. 'This too will pass'.

Chapter 20

Stella Trusts the Inner Critics Can Be Tamed

Sometimes holding myself
Is not enough
Sometimes having a warm bath
Is not enough
Sometimes touching myself
Is not enough
Sometimes I need someone
Being human is enough
Always

It is almost astounding how I every now and then put myself in a corner where I just do not have any chance against myself. Hitting hard, screaming loud, ending up like an old torn rag. Even though I see it, it is as if I cannot stop it. The same goes for how I do things that trigger pain and self-loathing, or how I do not do things I know will make me feel at ease, relaxed and content. At worst, I drive myself crazy and torture myself. I must be getting something out of it though, since I do seem to not stop, yet, but what? Is it the unconscious iceberg that lies behind this self-sabotage? Or is it, like someone said, just a cop-out, an excuse not to enjoy life? Then it is high bloody time that I stopped the torture and enjoyed the treasures I have been given.

It is also astonishing how quickly it can shift. I was feeling so good and had so much energy. I was efficient at work during the day, so left early, got home, did the Osho Kundalini Meditation and had a fruit salad followed by an unusually energetic walk to the movie theatre. What a turnaround. Maybe it was because it was in Spanish, a language I love and for which my teachers told me I had talent. However, a voice in me then says it's a talent I have wasted. Maybe it was Barcelona, a city I love and where I used to live. Maybe it was the friendship, the love. Maybe. Maybe it was all the chances I have not taken. Maybe it was a longing for touch, belonging, intimacy, sex. Maybe it was sadness for all those things not happening for such a long time, for a significant part of my life so far. Maybe. At times there is longing and sadness in me. There is love in me. There is joy in me. There is gratitude in me. There is trust in me. Trust! Things happen as they should and, luckily, the shift can go both ways.

"How many people would you say you trust?" Carl's question caught me a bit by surprise.

"How many people I trust? Ooops, well, I don't know. I think that depends on the circumstances and issue at hand."

"Do you trust me?" He looked at me inquiringly.

"Well, nowadays, yes, I'd say I do."

"Nowadays? So it hasn't always been like that?"

"Oh no, definitely not." I looked at him and smiled.

"That was quick."

"Yes, it was. I did not mean to hurt you, but when we were together in that, what we might call, intimate relationship of ours…"

I could still remember how insecure and jealous I often felt.

"You mean when we dated, had sex, lived together – and apart?"

"Yes, then I can honestly say that I didn't trust you fully. Did you trust me by the way?"

"Oh well, I think I did, more or less, at least more than you seem to have trusted me."

"I'd claim I had my reasons."

I realised a part of me wanted some kind of justification.

"You did, at least in the beginning." Carl acknowledged at least that much.

"And in the end."

"And in the end. Now I feel like an asshole."

"Ha, ha, maybe because you were. Sorry, but you handed me that one on a silver platter. But I do seem to remember moments when I got a glimpse of some jealousy in you too. Not that you had any reason; my God, I was so in love with you."

"Mmm, I was in love with you too."

"I do hope so, and I take your word for it – at least for a while there, in the beginning of the middle." I smiled at him.

"Exactly! After the very beginning, but before the end, and especially when you had baked cinnamon and vanilla buns. That I remember." Carl laughed, then became more serious and continued, "But the not-trusting and maybe jealousy. We did have a pretty difficult start in that sense."

"Yes, I still remember that fax – my goodness, we must be getting old. Does anyone know of, much less use fax machines anymore? Anyway, I guess it somehow created a basis for my mistrust in you. Then,

180

since I knew that that other friend of ours had a crush on you and did what she could; every time I knew you spent time together like at nights out, or when you went on business trips together, I was afraid you'd fall for her."

"Yeah, well, I didn't. But sometimes I had a feeling you saw ghosts everywhere and I remember that at some point I thought, 'what the hell I might as well go for it' with someone just to do it, since you anyway didn't believe me when I said there was nothing going on with anyone," Carl admitted.

"Mhmm. On that note, I heard somewhere that worrying is like praying for more of what you don't want. I guess I was a little paranoid. While we were together, did you ever get over the one before me?" Shit, I could have bitten my tongue off.

"You mean the one who moved? I chose to be with you didn't I? But in a way your suspicions were right; since she and I were never really together, a part of me was sometimes wondering how that would have been." Carl looked at his cup, then back at me.

"We had such a great relationshit, didn't we?" I smiled at him.

"You think so? Yes, I guess we did, and now maybe we have such a great relationship, because we're not in one? At least not of that kind."

"Yes, maybe, and it feels like this time we're really getting to know each other."

"Is that why you say that today you trust me?" Carl asked.

"I think it is at least part of why, and I guess that something has also shifted in me. But would you say there are different kinds of trust?" I had sometimes asked myself this.

"What do you mean?"

"I'm not sure, but I think I mean more like a general trust and a more specific trust." I hesitated.

"Like?"

"Like a general trust in life, let's say, and a more specific trust – or not – in certain people, people you know at least to some extent, in certain situations." I tried to explain as much to myself as to him.

"I think I understand what you mean. And well, yes, maybe there are…or maybe not; I mean, don't they go together?" Carl seemed to answer my question without really answering it.

"How do you mean? Do I hear you say that you don't think there are different kinds of trust? Or maybe I, or we, use 'trust' when other words would be more fitting or appropriate?"

"I'm thinking out loud here Stella, but if you have a general trust, doesn't that imply that you also trust people in general? Well, I guess until they have proven you wrong that is, then there might be a challenge to your trust…and vice versa; if you don't trust life, you also don't trust people. People are a big part of life."

Carl's reasoning did not leave much room for an opposing argument, at that moment.

"Indeed they – we – are and I see your point. And that would mean that until we can say that we trust people, anyone – and this could actually serve as a trust-thermometer – we don't fully trust. And by trusting life, I presume we mean seeing it as a basically benevolent force."

"Yes, I agree. When we trust someone, they usually stand up to that trust, even strangers. Take, for instance, when you're at an airport or a train station, travelling alone, and you need to go to the toilet but you cannot take your luggage with you, so you ask a stranger nearby if he is willing to keep an eye on it. In my experience, you usually get a smile and a yes, and when you come back it's still all there as you left it." Carl smiled.

"Yes, I've experienced that too. In this way, not only the question of how many people I trust, but also what I would trust with whom, kind of loses its significance."

I realised this trust subject had many aspects – and maybe not at its core.

"Maybe it does. So what would you say trust is, besides basically perceiving life as this benevolent force?"

"This is getting tricky – or perhaps not. If we bring in the concept of trustworthiness, whom do I find trustworthy? I think I'd say someone who stands his or her ground, who respects and cares about people, including me, who is honest, sincere, open…"

"I'm flattered." Carl was quick.

"Ha, ha, yes Carl, suck it up! Someone else would probably mention something else and possibly someone else would think of you differently."

"Nah…they couldn't, could they?"

"Of course not. We have the right answers, don't we?"

"No doubt about it."

"Our judgments and preconceptions seem to come in to play too. But it is interesting though."

"Yes?"

"Think of babies."

"What about them?" Carl asked.

"They are, we all were, these little feeling-bundles, totally dependent on our caretakers, usually mother and father to begin with, and full of trust. I mean, we wouldn't enter this world if in some way we didn't trust our needs would be taken care of, would we?"

"So you think we had a choice?"

"Who knows? Perhaps we did." I shrugged my shoulders.

"Ok, yeah, well, anyway, let's say that when we're born we're full of trust. Then what? We both know it doesn't continue quite like that, with humanity walking around as trusting beings," Carl asserted.

"No, unfortunately not. I guess life happens…" I lost the momentum for a moment.

"And boom, there goes life as a benevolent force down the drain," Carl said it in a way that made me think of a small boy.

"Yes, it's odd isn't it? I mean you could even stretch it as far as to say that we were all born with full trust, then as the years go by, we grow up and experience our different paths and, step-by-step, most of us lose trust, at least partially. Yet still we go on, so something must still be there." I had the feeling of venturing into unknown territory.

"All these brave little creatures. How come we do, do you think? Why do I? Why do you?"

"You know the saying about hope being the last thing that abandons us…"

"So we walk around hoping and searching for the return to that space and place full of trust?" Carl changed position and leaned back.

"Yeah, well, that could be one way of putting it."

"So how do we do it; what happens when that trust gradually disappears?"

"I don't know, but it seems like something else kicks in and takes the place of trust."

184

"And that would be?"

"That would be what we could call our ego and, not least, our superego. And now I have to go to the toilet."

"Ok, that's quite a cliff-hanger. You just leave me hanging here in suspense!"

"Be my guest."

I smiled and made my way to the ladies' room, sensing his thoughtful gaze at my back. When I returned, he was still looking quite preoccupied.

"You really had me hanging here."

"I did?"

"Yes, you did, and now it's my turn to go to the gents'." He smiled.

"Wow, that's what I call a quick return of favour. By the way, do you want something more?" I asked.

Carl quickly glanced at his watch.

"I really should be heading home soon, but I still have some time, so yes, just a refill please. We can't leave each other hanging until next week, can we?"

"Oh no, please! Off you go now!"

I went for some more coffee and Carl soon came back.

"So where were we? Ah yes, the superego. I can't really see the connection between trust and superego, so please enlighten me," Carl invited.

"So you mean to say you don't have one?"

"Oh no, according to your theory – and my practice and experience – I'm sure I do."

"Ok, I know I do too. So, the little baby grows up and takes her steps on this often rather bumpy road called life."

"And step-by-step, trust loses ground, which is taken up by the superego," Carl concluded.

"Something to that end."

"How? Why?"

"Well, we were all born fully open and trusting, entering a family, a community and a society where a certain language is spoken, which we learn. Then, we are expected to learn, understand and follow certain rules of behaviour if we want to be a part of and function in our family, community and society. And we do, since from the beginning we're totally dependent on our closest surroundings for our survival. We're also social beings who have a need to belong. In order to do that, most of us learn that all of our feelings, liveliness, spontaneity and impulses, cannot always be expressed as they surge, so we learn to suppress. We learn that not everything in us is always welcomed; that's usually just the way it is in the very beginning, and that's an intrinsic part of coming to this life. So, being these sensitive receptive beings, we soon learn under which conditions we will be welcomed, what we may express and how we should behave in order to belong. Sometimes we're being told and at other times we just perceive it; very often words are not needed, because children sense and notice anyway."

"In the air or atmosphere," Carl added.

"Exactly. Soon we don't have to be told, as soon these voices and vibes are internalised, telling us what to do and what not to do."

"The superego."

"That's one name for it; the inner critic or judge are the other names. While you were gone, this little graph came to me; I remember, you like diagrams and stuff like that."

"You do?" He smiled in surprise. "Yes, I guess I still do. So please show me."

"I will."

I took out a notepad and a pencil from my bag.

"It's something like this."

I drew a diagram to illustrate what I had tried to put into words.

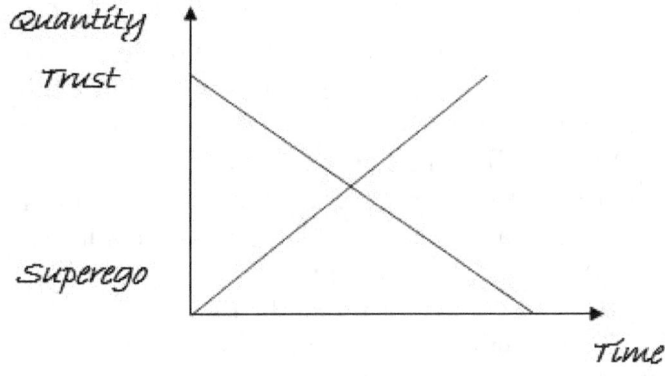

"Hey, I like that! Makes it very clear. Maybe a bit oversimplified, but that's of course the nature of these diagrams and models."

"I'm glad you like it."

"So what can we do to change the curves?"

When Carl asked, I could easily imagine him at his business meetings.

"Oh, I wish I had a simple answer to that."

"You don't? I'm disappointed!" Carl laughed.

"Ha, ha, I am too."

"But at least I trust you must have one little idea or two?" He blinked. "You don't want me to lose hope, do you?"

"No, I most certainly don't and I don't want to lose hope either."

"So?"

"So…my hope is that the first step out of the reign of the superego is to see it and to become aware of it. Then you can ask yourself how much of it is really your truth in your life of today as a more or less independent adult. If it is your truth, then fine. If it's not, then if you want, maybe you can find an alternative way of behaving, or at least start exploring the alternatives."

"Sounds like another piece of cake."

"I'm not saying it's easy; then again, trying it out might gradually make it easier and we might discover something else, something new."

"Or quite old?" Carl remarked.

"Yes, right, that which was there from the beginning, but became buried."

"So, slowly we can uncover trust again. By seeing and stepping out of the unwanted – or no longer needed – opinions and advice of the superego, and autopilot of the ego or mind, we can come back to trusting ourselves, others and life. Stella…?"

"Yes?"

"There is this voice in me telling me I'd better leave. My superego now finds himself in double, or maybe it's even triple loyalties here."

"Possibly even more if you look carefully." I smiled.

"You're probably right."

"So what will happen if you don't obey the voice that tells you to leave?"

"I'll probably be home later than I said, feel ashamed and guilty about it and apologise to Donna. And hope she will forgive me." Carl crossed his fingers.

"There you go!"

"What?"

"First of all, one of the workings of the superego: Not obeying often makes us feel ashamed."

"Well, ok, and I know nicer feelings."

"Me too, and that's one thing we learned. Not obeying means shame and possibly also punishment of some kind, which we want to avoid, so we learn to obey in order not to feel that. And then there's also guilt if we do something that we think will be perceived as not so nice to someone else. Fear too is one; keeping us from expressing ourselves, from trying new ways and things, preferably staying in the comfort zone and often ending up frustrated or bored."

"Or both…or even depressed." Carl added.

"Very likely and notwithstanding all of that, with a little distance to it, the superego could also have the function of a guide. You either follow his advice because it holds something you value, or you don't because it doesn't."

"That's the knack right, getting that distance? Do you have some more tricks to share? Checking if what he claims still holds true is one, saying 'no' or 'stop' I guess would be another?"

"Absolutely and, as always, injecting some humour could also help, as could lovingly thanking him, since he got me this far after all. I also see that even if I may have been a slave under his out-dated rule many times,

189

I did my best, and he wanted my best. For all of it, my universal medicine is meditation. We could probably come up with more."

"That's all very good. Also just talking about it I'd assume, which would need some more time, but I really have to go now." Carl had another look at his watch.

"Yes, you'd better, and I ought to too."

"Can I give you a ride or do you have your car?" Carl asked.

"Thank you for offering. No, I don't have the car, but I prefer to walk. I feel I need some air and I also enjoy a bit of exercise."

"Ok, fair enough."

We hugged goodbye and he left. I watched his back, finding myself alone again, but not lonely. I remembered an explanation from school about aloneness being more the physical state of not being with company, and loneliness more the psychological state of missing 'company'. Later, I had heard Osho say something like 'Loneliness is the absence of the other. Aloneness the presence of oneself', which resonated with me, and I had also experienced the feeling that loneliness is just as much the absence of myself in some sense as the absence and the missing of the other. For most of us, regarding company – our own and others – it is probably the fact that it is not infinite, that it has a beginning and an end, that we get it in doses and in some kind of flow between the two – being alone and being together – that makes both enjoyable. Experiencing only one would presumably drive many of us crazy to some extent.

As much as I enjoy this time with Carl and others, I also enjoy time with myself. In fact, time with myself is a must, as is time with others, particularly of course people I love and care about and with whom I feel it is reciprocated.

I was heading home for a nice, warm bath, some relaxing music and, later, a meditation to complete the day. Freedom. Connection. I like!

Chapter 21

Carl Makes Do Without a Contingency Plan, and It is All Same Same, but Different

What is the difference
Between me and me?
You? Life?
We are life.
So what difference does it make?
What difference do we make?

"Stella, please remind me that I often tell you how much I like my job and the people I work with and have working for me!"

"Why, what happened?" Stella looked at me with surprise.

"Later, now please just…" I carelessly pulled the chair out and sat down with a deep sigh.

"Ok, ok! Carl, I'm so happy you took the time to come today, since you have so often told me how much you like what you do, and how the people you're working with are such a competent and fun bunch to have around."

"Thank you. As strange as it might seem, I really needed to hear that."

"That much I understood and if you'd like to explain why, feel free," Stella invited.

"Well, you know, it's been one of those days when nothing seems to work, so seeing you today feels more welcome than ever and is what I think has kept me from creating even more havoc by being the worst boss ever, raging against everything and everyone."

"So being here is a good thing, because the rest of the day has been less than so?"

"Yes, I guess these kind of days are inevitable sometimes and maybe also needed as a contrast."

"That may be so, but you still have a rather curious woman in front of you," Stella admitted.

"To begin with, our morning routines at home did not run very smoothly today. Eric did not want to get up and turned out to have a fever, Flore did not want to get dressed, then did not want to have breakfast and, of course, did not want to go to pre-school. Donna and I had an argument, or we might as well call it a fight, about whether it was more important for me or her to be at work today. Since I'm running my own company with employees and we're usually involved in business deals that are very important – not least to our clients – I usually win those fights, like I did this morning."

"In addition, you bring in more money than she does, but you were not feeling the need to bring that one up, since it's rather obvious."

"Yes, well, that's how it is; no need to point that out every time."

"Of course not. So we can say you won that battle, but the war is not yet over, huh? And the boss was not very happy and relaxed when he entered the office this morning."

"No, you could say that."

"So, what happened at work?"

"The major thing was that one of our biggest clients suddenly told us that they wanted to pull out of a merger that we've been working on quite intensively for the last six months. And, of course, the senior consultant in charge is laid up with pneumonia or something. Who knows why or how it happened, but it was as if everyone and everything was affected by panic, including computers and printers. I soon got the impression that nothing and no one could stand up to what I would call normal functioning." I shook my head at the thought.

"It sounds like a tough setback to me. What did you do?"

"For a while I'd say I was one of the erring crowd, but one of the first things I did, of course, was to have a talk with the client. No final decisions have been made yet; maybe they just got cold feet and need some time to adjust to the new ideas and settings. The deal has been put on hold for two weeks, then we'll see." I made a symbolic cross over my chest.

"You sound pretty together and almost optimistic."

"Well, I still think this is a not only a good, but even a necessary deal and merger for them, and somehow I am convinced that they will come to that conclusion too."

"And if they don't, you will lose a lot of money?"

"More than I would like to, obviously, but it should not be in the range of endangering bankruptcy."

"That's a relief, to say the least. Just a temporary change of subject; they seem to expect us to order something," Stella observed.

"Oh, yes of course. I'll have the usual…no, wait please, today I want regular coffee with a piece of William's cake."

"Ok, that's interesting – and maybe inspiring." She smiled. "And if they don't have William's?"

"Hmm…a frog."

"Ok, let's see what I come back with."

A few minutes later she came back with two pieces of cake and the obligatory coffees.

"I figured this could be a day you wouldn't mind having some of both, so have as much as you want of the frog and I'll have the rest. Apparently, I still haven't given up on them...ha, ha."

"Ha, ha, good, you shouldn't. But I'm afraid this one will be a disappointment, if it is a prince you're looking for."

"What a pity. Maybe I can ask them to create a Prince's cake to complement the Princess's. It would be about time by the way, or maybe there is one already?" Stella speculated.

"Not that I know of."

"Maybe next time. Now, where were we? Ah yes; so there is no bankruptcy in sight, even if that deal doesn't go through?"

"Right. It's been a very interesting day in many ways though. It feels like I learned a lot, both about myself, my staff and the client; that is, about our reactions and behaviour in this situation," I reflected.

"I'm sure you did and I would like to hear about it."

"I'll start with me. Like you said, I was pretty stressed out already when I arrived and I had just hung up my coat, when the second consultant showed up, pale in the face, and delivered the news. My first reaction was that I got so bloody angry with him. Luckily I managed to contain some of that anger, but I was not very friendly when I asked him to come with me to my office and tell me all he knew. My secretary was on the receiving end of some of it too, as was everyone else who got in my way on my way out."

I paused for some cake.

"On your way out?"

"Yes, when 'junior' was finished, I sat for a few moments and felt I had to move and get some air, so I told my secretary that I'd be back in an hour or so and asked her to tell everyone to continue with their work as usual. Perhaps not the smartest decision, but that's what I did. I took the car to the forest, did some screaming, walked around, jumped up and down, threw some cones, touched the trees, the bushes, got some fresh air in my system…what??"

Her happy expression diverted my attention.

"No, no, please continue. I'll tell you later."

"Ok. So, when I felt I had calmed down and had something of a plan clear to me, I went back to the car and returned to the office. When I arrived, the smell of panic and things being in a mess struck me, so I called everyone together for a meeting. Luckily, I had brought a bunch of buns and pastry as a peace offering. I briefed them about the situation, and asked what was going on for each one of them. After that, it felt as though we could get back to work again, without having to kick the copying machine or each other."

"Honestly, Carl, without having been there, it sounds to me like you did brilliantly today. Here; have the frog too! Or what's left of it." Stella pushed the small plate towards me.

"Thank you. When I came back though, I sensed that leaving like I did made them feel as though the captain had abandoned the ship or something, but I really needed to get out. In hindsight, maybe it wasn't so stupid after all." I was more or less thinking out loud.

"Like I said, and for whatever it's worth, I think you did great."

"What was that smile about, then?"

I had not forgotten and would not let her off the hook.

"Oh that. It was your need to scream, to move, to really express all those emotions and energy that were obviously building up inside, which is so much healthier and more natural than our usual, learned way of repressing it so it gets stuck in the body. And also how you connected with the trees, bushes, nature. Do you remember how that made you feel?"

"It actually felt really good, a release, easy, all of it. I even hugged and talked to a beautiful, tall birch tree, and it almost felt like it talked to me too, like we were the same. Shit, what is this? You did not hear me say that!"

"I did, but it stays between us like always." Stella smiled, and blinked. "Don't worry. Just enjoy this moment of being one with everything. At least that is what it sounds like to me."

"I'd say you're spot on. And since you are, I guess you have had similar experiences?"

"Yes, I think I have."

"What was so surprising to me, was that when I came back to that relative chaos in the office, I still felt relaxed. Even though it was not quite according to how I had planned the rest of the day on my way back, every step flowed, and it also felt like the others could relax and see things more clearly. All in all, I think it was one of our worst and best days so far."

"Wow!"

"Yeah! Wow! Let me get us some more coffee. I would like to hear a little from you if you still have time." I made a move to stand up.

197

"I do, but wait, actually, I'd rather have a glass of wine and something a bit salty."

"Ok, that sounds good to me. Let's move next door then and see if they'll have us."

"Yes, that's a very good idea. I really like that place."

Next door was a nice, cosy Italian restaurant and since we were both regular customers and it was a weekday, they'd hopefully let us have some wine and something light to eat. They did, so we continued, now each with a glass of Vino Nobile di Montepulciano and some antipasti, bread and olive oil with a slightly grassy and peppery taste, with some grains of sea salt sprinkled in it.

"It's not all that easy to continue with all of this in front of me."

"I agree, but since we're going to be here for a while, let's enjoy it all as it comes. Cheers!" I lifted my glass and looked her in the eyes.

"You're right. Cheers!"

"So, let me hear some of your management mysteries, please."

"Myths Marking the Middle Management Morass, maybe." Stella seemed to have something coming to mind.

"Alliteration, mmm, I like that," I commented, as I rolled the glass a little and with a long, soft intake of breath, smelled the wine, exhaled with contentment and took a sip of wine. It was to my taste.

"Yes, you see what inspiration the moment can bring. Anyway, what I recall immediately are two situations, although there could probably be more. One is when I was the number two with a very visionary number one. I found myself being the 'boring one', keeping track of laws and regulations, asking her why and how she had planned to finance, or go through with, this or that idea. I kept us kind of anchored to the reality of our operating situation. I was also the one dealing with the nitty-gritty of everyday issues and challenges in the office and with our staff, partners and clients, which could sometimes feel quite trivial when the director was full on in her visions. Both are needed and the people who do the job need to stay motivated and focused. We usually found our way as we went along and the company grew, both in terms of turnover and number of employees, with a solid core.

"The other is when I was working for the big international, prestigious organisation I may have told you about. I worked in a division that was given different missions and projects in what sometimes felt like God-forsaken places. I was responsible for groups ranging from about 10 to 30 people – men and women aged 30-60+ – from all over the world. Some were at the start of their careers, whilst others were looking forward to retirement. All had been the chosen ones in their countries and had their CVs, competencies, positions, ambitions – and pretty strong personalities. Luckily, all were committed and willing though. I guess we all felt we were there to support a good cause with our work."

"And you were in charge?"

"Yes. Of course, I had superiors to report to. As you know there is a big overhead administration at the headquarters from where we get our projects, missions, goals and budgets, but it was my job to organise these 'task forces' and see to it that the work was completed in a professional and timely fashion, with the goals and clients' needs, experiences and benefits as our main target, within budget, of course." Stella gave an outline of the job description.

"It sounds to me like you must have had your hands full and your fair share of challenges."

"Well, I have to admit that there were moments when I asked myself what on Earth I was doing there and why, and considered my options, but I also had a lot of fun. As you said earlier, I felt that I learned a lot about myself and other people. But sure, one example of challenges you face when trying to get everything to function together – and sometimes on a fairly basic and hands on level – is when time is limited, there's a lot to do and some people don't deliver on time, for various reasons." Stella opened her palms.

"So what did you do?"

"Ha, ha, well…I don't know what I 'did' really, or whether it was that much. Maybe dropped some of my ideas to begin with, making do with what was. You know; what you probably do all the time too."

"Well, I'm not so sure about that, but we will find out if you elaborate a bit more." I would not let her get away that easily.

"Ok. On a practical level in both these examples and with the smaller groups, we occasionally had informal, semi-formal or formal meetings or, depending on the situation, maybe lunch or dinner together, just to give us all the opportunity to connect with each other. We were often scattered around in different places, basically communicating on the phone, so these meetings helped us to gain a feeling for the teams and tasks involved and to address or share whatever was needed, since the circumstances could sometimes be quite challenging and trigger all kinds of reactions, as happened with you today. When I felt the need, another thing was to remind us all of why we were 'there', and emphasise the need to stay focused on our priorities, so that we could all hopefully understand, remember and be motivated by that. I was also rather surprised by how relaxed I felt and how I was not overly fixated on so many ideas I might have had. Knowing how I was before, with perfectionist traits and, when overstressed, possibly tense and rigid, I felt like I could stand my ground. With a bit of authority when needed, I was able to explain how I saw the missions and tasks, the structures needed, explain why I considered certain details important and get most of the team to understand, acknowledge and agree to this, while we were also having fun together. It felt rather easy and relaxed, which the teams largely seemed to have felt too, at least according to the feedback I received." Stella paused and had a sip of water and wine before she continued.

"In short, and as I put it in one of the reports that was required, it primarily boiled down to three 'r's happening in their own time and order: relating, rewarding and relaxing. It helps to have a cool head, a warm heart, hands ready to work and feet on the ground." Stella summarised with a mischievous smile. All of a sudden she burst out with amusement, "Ha, ha, for heaven's sake, tell me to shut up! I really do sound like one of those pompous reports."

"Ha, ha, why should I? This is interesting!"

"Honestly, hearing what I just said feels like an afterthought, or whatever; a lot of words to say about which I actually have no idea, even though I did go through all the red tape and did write the expected reports and summaries about it. It happened; I was just there." She shrugged her shoulders.

"That's something that might be worth remembering; the r's I mean. It should be possible even for my memory to grasp and store, if you don't mind," I emphasised, holding up three fingers in the air and emitting a quiet whistle, whilst silently repeating them to myself. "And what you call 'just being there' probably plays a more important role than your putting it in a subordinate clause would suggest. I am just wondering how you formulated that in your reports?"

"Ha, ha, that's a good point. I appreciate your opinion. Anyway, 'r's or not, to be honest I'm not so convinced that that kind of work, as in relating or parenting or whatever you want to call it, can be boiled down to a simple recipe or manual or something to that end. It's like love, meditation and life as such; it cannot be described really, it needs to be experienced and we all experience things in our own way, so I can only share my own experiences. It was a great one; they all were, in different ways, but with certain common denominators – not least this thing with communication, which is really something. I mean, even if or when we don't have the language skills as such to consider, what I say – or what I think I say – and what you hear is very often not the same thing, since we all have our different filters and much of the time actually have a tendency to give different meanings and weight to words and expressions, not to mention our degree of attention," Stella remarked.

"I have noticed that more than once, both at home and at work. It's surprisingly easy to forget though. As is the fact that what we say with words is one thing, and often less important than how we say it and what we transfer with body language etc."

"It is. By the way, from the experiences I mentioned – and others too – it has become obvious to me how meditation helps me to cope in situations involving responsibility, long-term stress, lots of people, expectations and demands, frustration, different cultures and conditionings and, at times, not very familiar physical and technical circumstances and conditions. It has also become apparent how different and unique we all are, and at the same time so alike, so much the same; not separate, but all one. Meditation allows me and 'issues' to move, to watch them, and not get overly stuck in too many internal or external dramas about being inadequate or hopeless and instead see things as they are and go with that, with me being a 'tool'. It also gives me my own time and space."

Stella closed her eyes for a moment, took a few long, soft breaths and nodded. She opened her eyes, looked at me, nodded again, and had some of the bread and wine.

"On the topic of internal and external communication, this wine is really good!"

"Yes, I like it too; a lot. It's quite velvety and still has a lot of taste." I smelled the wine, took another sip, and let it linger in the mouth for some moments to see what the taste buds could identify. "To me it has a hint of black cherries …some plum… some leather…"

"Mhmm, and also some cocoa… some mint and some oak. Anyway, like we said, really good!" Stella joined in in the appreciation of the Tuscan nectar.

"Maybe I bring my hedonism into blasphemy here, but actually, the differences in taste, colour, fragrance this wine has, also bring different qualities and a richness to the experience, just like a group of people, or individuals in a team do." I heard the phone beep and checked it. "Ooops, time flies when we're having fun. Let's see how velvety the family welcome will be." I took a last sip.

"Ha, ha, creative observation, blasphemous or not. You have talked to Donna during the day, haven't you?"

"Yes, I have. We worked it out. She was ok and knows I will be a bit late."

"Good. Let's hope everybody is well tomorrow."

"Oh yes! Can I give you a ride home by the way?"

"Oh, thank you, that would be great. To be honest, I don't feel like walking in this weather."

I would not usually drive after having had a beer or a glass of wine, but the glass was quite small and I had not even finished it, so this once I thought it was ok. It had been in a way a special day – and at the same time not so different from any other day. It was like the lyrics from a Phil Collins' song: 'another day in paradise', with all these people, all these situations and all these experiences in what we call life. Life as we know it; as good as it gets.

Chapter 22

Stella's Hellish Pain Reminds Her of Heaven

Light
Light without
Light within
Ephemeral
Perpetual
We are that
Light

"Hi Carl, I'm sorry I'm late."

"Hi Stella! Don't worry; that's totally fine. I just got here too. Our timing seems to be pretty well in tune. Maybe we could also say that we are in tune with each other these days."

"Yes, I agree, I think we could. That's good, isn't it?" I carefully sat down in the sofa with a deep sigh. "Good to finally get to sit down and be here with you too."

"Absolutely. Coffee for you?"

"Yes, the usual blend with milk, please. And a cinnamon bun."

"Aha?"

"Please. I'll tell you."

"Ok, now you have me wondering."

"Oh come on, because of a cinnamon bun?"

"That and something else I'm going to tell you."

"Ok, we're even. Now, off you go!" I laughed.

Carl winked as he walked away. I managed to remove my coat and found a seat where I hoped I would look natural and relaxed, but I was not so sure. My body was reminding me of its presence, and had not been up to its normal standard for a couple of days. Carl came back with our coffees, my bun and a few more goodies.

"So, what's happening?" Carl asked as he sat down again.

"You mean, why do I leave my so-called self-discipline aside and give into the craving for a bun?"

"Yes, it got me wondering, and you don't look as relaxed as you usually do."

"Hmm, you're becoming amazingly attentive, or else I'm a lousy actor!" I laughed.

"Let's say it's a combination then, but apparently I'm onto something."

"Yes, well…yes. I am comfort eating."

"That's obvious." Carl smiled. "Should I be worried? Is there something serious troubling you?"

"No, I don't think you need to worry, not yet anyway, but please remind me not to make this a habit."

"Ok, if you say so. And? I did see your grimaces you know."

I laughed, which made me grimace again, and more so.

"See? There we go again. Pain?" Carl asked, a little concerned.

"Yes, but only when I laugh."

Neither of us could help but laugh, which almost made me cry from the pain.

"The pain is obvious."

"And when I move and breathe," I added, almost panting.

"They say that laughter makes you live longer, so you'd better laugh to offset what the pain indicates...but Stella, it really doesn't look good to me."

"It's mainly the left lung, or at least mostly in that area."

"The lung; not that serious then, huh? For heaven's sake, have you been checked for this?" Carl asked with concern.

"No, I haven't. I mean, not now. I don't think there's much that can be done about it anyway. It feels like when I had pleurisy a few years ago, so my guess is that that is what it is."

"Ah, the almost-doctor speaking. And what did the real doctor do at the time?"

"Some adjustments to my medication and advised me to take it easy, so..."

"So you mean to say that's what you do now too?"

"More or less, yes."

"Mamma mia, I'm happy I'm not your doctor." Carl shook his head.

"She probably is. I mean, she's busy enough without me there more often than necessary."

"And when would you say is 'necessary'?" Carl inquired.

"When they want to see me, or when I feel I have to, I guess. I mean 'have to' in the sense that I think or hope there might be something they can do, other than just telling me to rest or 'wait and see'. One usually has to be pretty patient to be a patient. Maybe that's why it's called patient?"

"Maybe. Aren't you ever afraid? I mean, knowing you, when you make grimaces and hold yourself like that, it must really hurt and the lungs are of vital importance."

"I suppose I do get afraid, but then again, not really. I mean it is the way it is and I want to do what I can while I can, since I have been reminded that sooner or later I will not be able to do…whatever, or most of what people our age would generally do without giving it a thought. That status quo cannot be taken for granted, which I tend to forget sometimes. I think one of my biggest fears is not being able to take care of myself and to end up bitter and lonely in some kind of institution or hospital. You know; we've been into this one before."

This was not my favourite subject, and yet acknowledging it made it less frightening.

"I would probably have those fears too. And others. But isn't it amazing how we seem to need those rather harsh reminders to remember?"

"Yes; it's pretty sad in a way – or maybe not. Maybe those who don't get the reminders, don't need to be reminded, because they remember anyway?"

"I have my doubts, but ok, who knows?" Carl was obviously not convinced.

"One good thing about pain that you believe will pass, is that it reminds you how good it is not to have pain. I also realise that there have been periods in my life when pain was there all the time, like I told you, when almost every little movement and touch hurt and somehow I just kept going. Imagine the amount of energy that must have taken, and how on Earth could I function as well as I did?"

Looking back, I was quite astonished myself.

"Yes, that's really something, all of it. How did you?"

"To be honest, I don't know – and one day, I didn't anymore."

"I was almost going to say 'thank heaven for that'. You are human you know."

"Ha, ha, very much so I'd say! But having no pain is not to be taken for granted, even though most of us have a tendency to do that. Me too, admittedly, until some pain hits again and I am reminded."

Sometimes, one also needs to analyse whether there might be something behind the pain, I thought to myself.

"Unfortunately."

"Not having pain really is such a gift and gives you so many opportunities to do whatever you can, or in the best of situations, want to do. Well, actually the possibilities are always there, just a bit different, given different circumstances."

"Maybe it really isn't about what we have, but what we do with it, or something similar, which my grandmother used to say. It seems to have its truth and become relevant here."

"Yes, I agree, I think it does. I mean, if we take one day, any day, we usually have plans, but honestly, whether it's going to be a good day, or a bad day, is really up to us."

"You say honestly. Do you honestly really think so?" Carl seemed to have his doubts again.

"Yes, basically I do, but admittedly I don't always live or act accordingly. I think it was Buddha who said that it is our minds that create our reality. And yes, it is what we think about something that decides what we feel about it, isn't it?"

209

"What I hear you're saying is that there is no absolute or intrinsic 'good' or 'bad', but our thoughts and interpretations about things that decide?" Carl clarified.

"Yes, many have put it that way and there seems to be something to it, wouldn't you agree? Of course there are situations where this might seem difficult to apply, like when children fall seriously ill and so on, but we could ask ourselves every morning, 'What do I want today; heaven or hell?'"

"Well, when you put it like that, the choice is obvious, isn't it? Yet still so many of us have this tendency to create hell for ourselves so much of the time."

"Mhmm, we do, but once we see it, change can begin to happen, don't you think?"

"I certainly do hope so."

"Me too. I keep reminding myself, when I realise that the hellish programme is running the show."

"Realising it is a good start, I'd say. For whatever reason, these old sayings just run through my head." Carl raised his eyebrows.

"Which ones?"

"You know: 'Today is the first day of the rest of your life' and 'All those days that passed, I didn't realise that was life', or something similar."

"Yes, I know them too." I looked at him. "They may be called platitudes and sound trivial, but as usual with these things they really do carry a message if you take them in, don't they? I mean, we could make life something quite abstract if we stick to planning the future, or thinking about the past, or wishing things could be different, all of which many of us spend a lot of time doing."

"We seem to do that, yes," Carl agreed.

"And things actually are the way they are. Accepting that, instead of fighting it, or dwelling on it, would save us quite a lot of energy and time that we could use to enjoy the 'here and now', to change what can be changed and accept what cannot."

"You mean like lighting a light instead of complaining about the dark?" He smiled at me and continued. "And that's another one."

"It is. And speaking of heaven or hell, light and dark, however trite we may find it, when push comes to shove, there really is no way around it; how we spend our days is how we spend our lives."

"Ouch! So you mean I'd better stop planning?" He winked.

"Well, that's perhaps taking it a bit far. Some things need planning for sure, but the important thing is not to forget to enjoy the present. And the present might sometimes involve planning for the future."

"Ah yes, like choosing where to go on holiday and make the reservations…mmm," Carl said, rather dreamily.

"For instance that, yes. Where are you going?"

"Our next trip will be to Italy."

"Wonderful. Where to? It's a pretty big country with a lot to offer."

"It is. The Amalfi Coast, Sorrento and around."

"Mmmm, mi piace! Can I come?" I joked.

"Sure, that's actually a good idea! Why don't you join us?"

"Yeah, why don't I? Well, I don't know, that would perhaps be stretching it a bit far. I'm sure Donna would be thrilled." I smiled at the thought. "When are you going?"

211

"In April, over Easter."

"That sounds like a good way of getting a taste of real spring or even summer, if you're lucky with the weather."

"Yes, and good food and wine and…la dolce vita."

"Mmm…yes, the best, and speaking of food and the earlier subject, our thoughts…"

"Yes, are you by any chance taking us away from Italy now?" Carl protested.

"Only briefly if you don't mind, since something crossed my mind."

"Ok?"

"We've kind of touched on this several times already…" I felt some hesitation building up.

"Yes?"

"What we eat affects how we're doing, right?"

"Yes."

"And what we think also affects how we're doing. Our thoughts can be regarded as nourishment for the mind, like food is nourishment for the body."

And love and what we find beautiful and joyous is nourishment for the soul, I noted mentally.

"I'm with you."

"Another aspect is that our thoughts also affect the body, and the body affects our thoughts. So this is to say that…"

"…Psyche and soma go together, and there's nowhere better to go than Italy in April! See you there!" Carl's conclusion emphasised his point.

"I'll see what I can come up with. If I manage it, we could at least meet for dinner at some point."

"Yes, that would be great. Salute!"

212

Going to Italy again was a strong possibility, as was going to many other beautiful places. Going with Carl and his family would most likely not happen, for other reasons. No matter what, when, or where, there is one whose company is always there – my own. That is really 'for better or worse, in sickness and health, till death do us part'. How I spend my days, in this body, in my company – is up to me. It may be heaven or hell, dull and dark or fun and light. It all has its space, regardless of place.

Chapter 23

Carl Figures Out That He Cannot Figure It Out, but Does So Anyway

Wanting to do Something
but what?
Wanting to go Somewhere
but where?
Wanting to live Somehow
but how?
Wanting to love Someone
but who?
There is no but
No what
No where
No how
No who
Being here now
Will do

"Do you think there is a difference between longings, or maybe what we call dreams, and desire?" Stella's question had me a little confused.

"I sometimes feel like a broken record; what do you mean?"

"Ha, ha, what I mean...I guess I think I mean, do you differentiate between desire and longing?"

"I don't know...I haven't really thought about it."

"I kind of have..." She gave me that quick, a little awkward smile she sometimes does. "In doing so, I realised I have been using the words as if they mean the same thing and actually I don't think they do. At least not to me, not anymore, not when I give it some thought."

"Ok. Tell me and I might think about it too."

"Well, what I used to call longing, such as longing for ecstatic moments, enjoying a glass of good wine, spicy food, the sensation of tears, waking up feeling alert, falling in love, experiencing mutual infatuation and love, or for fulfilling sex again, is really just the mind's, or ego's or even body's desire for more."

"Really? And?"

"Yes...as I see it; at least sometimes." She almost excused herself. "What difference would it actually make? I have already experienced it. Well, except maybe the mutual infatuation and love."

I must have given her a look.

"Sorry, that was meant as a joke." Stella smiled and continued. "And I feel gratitude for having had those experiences. If it happened again, there would hopefully be awareness of it and enjoyment in the moment – and then what? Probably a desire for more, since the mind is apparently never satisfied. And here now, what is really the problem? Unless I give importance to mind-fucking? Everything is the way it is; the body, sex, relationships...and life is good the way it is, with loving friends, work, meditation and relative health. I need to look beyond all that I don't have, all that I can't do; to enjoy what I actually can do, what I do have, and see that there is more than the body, more than the ego-mind, more than sensual pleasure and enjoyment. On top of that, sensual pleasure and enjoyment are still available, are still there, but just not triggered by as many, or the same, stimuli as before."

"Wow, you really have been thinking about this, haven't you?"

"I don't know if there was so much thinking actually, but anyway, it came to me. And you know, I still get touched and I still cry, even if the visible signs like tears no longer surface."

"I don't know where that came from, but it shows and you know that."

"Yeah...I guess I do – and it does, at least if one knows about it. However, I sometimes think it would be nice to feel tears on my cheeks at some point again. My eyes probably would be more contented too, but if I don't, then so be it. Anyway, leaving tears or no-tears behind, if I no longer have the idea that the pleasure from a good Amarone, for example, is greater or better than the pleasure from a glass of water..."

I smirked. Stella noticed of course.

"Yes, water does taste differently; haven't you noticed?" she asked.

"If you say so. No, alright, I have, and we discussed that not so long ago, if you recall."

"I do. The Amarone and water; if I don't have that idea, then neither the longing that I would rather call desire, frustration, disappointment, or sadness will be there."

"Wouldn't that be boring?"

"Maybe it would if you're attached to feeling bad!" She smiled teasingly. "I see it more like a greater openness to enjoying what is, instead of wishing things were different. Of course, I sometimes do wish things were different. I do feel desire sometimes and when it does, I just notice it, feel it, am with it, enjoy it…and maybe have it satisfied, if possible."

"Sounds easy. Does it work?" I wondered.

"Well…yes, sometimes it does." That smile again. I just loved it.

"I have to tell you; I just love your smile."

"Oh, really? Thank you." She smiled even more.

"Mhmm. So, you're not saying that you don't have desires anymore? Or that desires are bad?"

"No! Of course not." Stella laughed. "I'm still very human with an active ego and mind, and bodily needs and preferences, so like I said, I do desire things sometimes – or, quite often to be honest. All I can say to that is, for example, a fresh chocolate praline like Manon Noir from Neuhaus. If I'm lucky enough to stay alert, I may be able to drop some of the desires, if I find them destructive. Hopefully, I will be able to use that energy to do something constructive instead, maybe with my longings."

"Now you're talking. What about those longings? What are they, if not something you want more of, if you don't mind my asking?"

"Good question, and no, I don't mind."

"So?" I insisted.

"I'm still a bit curious about this one too. It feels like, what I would refer to as longings are more difficult to express, to put in words, which could be because they're somehow beyond words."

Intentionally or not, Stella let the words linger.

"Oh come on, don't play esoteric with me now!" I blurted out.

"I'm not! I'm just erring a bit, since it is to me like something that doesn't come from thinking or the intellect, and words are thought-products, aren't they?

217

You know me, I can be quite a word-person; one of all these contradictions in me. So what can I say about longings? Maybe they stand for something inside that wants to be expressed and shared, and desires stand for something I want to have, to get?"

"Ok, but I'm not so sure I get it yet. What about the law of attraction, with its notion that we receive what we intend and wish for – consciously or unconsciously – on one side and us taking responsibility for our lives and how we live on the other? I think there's some kind of connection, different sides or not."

"Let's see…you mean like when we don't do what we know would be good for us, or postpone, or prioritise simpler – but perhaps less important – things, which have the tendency to create inner and bodily tension, or what?"

"Something like that I guess…and setting goals and working our way towards them," I added.

"Maybe we come back to the fact that we are so much run by our unconscious, that a presumably conscious decision is overruled by our unconscious that usually wants to stay in the comfort zone, and tends to follow the path of least resistance," Stella mused.

"Could be. Any ideas how we could strengthen ourselves in this context?" I held my hopes high.

"Hmm, I don't know, but as usual, perhaps being aware of this mechanism is the first step, reminding ourselves about where we want to go a second step and somehow making the benefits clear could be next."

"Sounds reasonable. Would you have something a bit more concrete to add?"

"It's funny, you're the one who used to come up with models and now I actually have a little something coming to mind." Stella smiled.

"Please show me. Do you need a piece of paper?"

"It's ok, thank you, I have some." She took out a notebook and a pen from her bag. "What do you think about this?" She drew an outline on a page in her book and turned it to me.

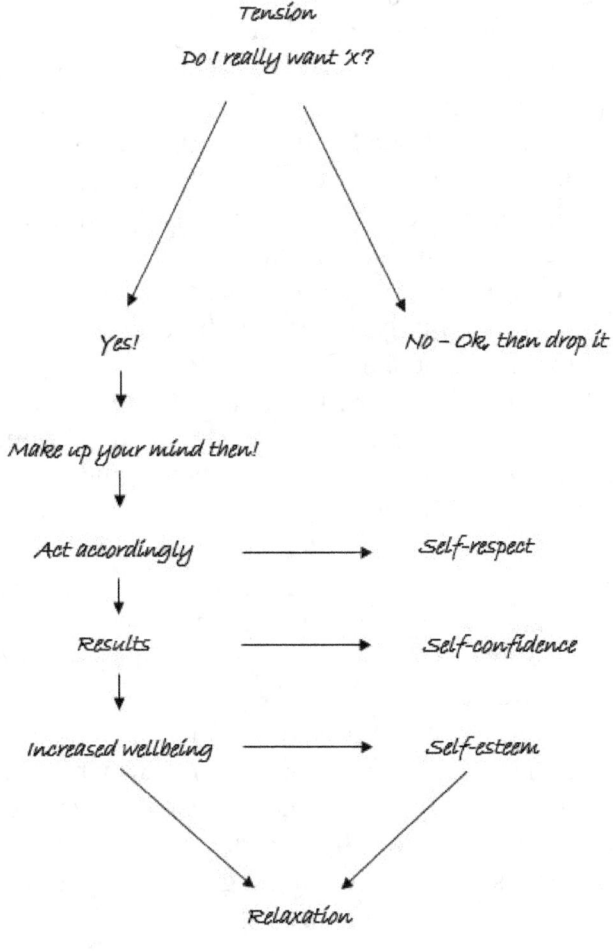

"Interesting…"

"Hmm, thank you for that one. That's really a word that usually means quite the opposite. Anyway, it could of course be elaborated on, but do you see what I mean? Do you think this is helpful?"

"I do. I might even put it on the fridge if that's ok with you?"

I found her model quite astute, but for some reason I did not tell her that. I wondered why.

"Of course, but why on the fridge might I ask?"

"Because there I would see it every day. And it might be a good reminder when I'm about to get something out of bad habit rather than hunger."

I had had this tendency for far too long now.

"Ok. They sound like perfectly good reasons. I might do the same." Stella smiled.

"Alright. Do you have magnets or could I have the honour of bringing you one next time?"

"I would appreciate it if you did."

"Ok, I will. I'd better make a note lest I should forget." I picked up my phone and added a reminder in the calendar. "Isn't it a bit contradictory though?"

"What is?" Stella asked.

"I mean, we've been talking more than once about acceptance and being with what is, being in the here now, and if you compare that to desires, longings, dreams and fulfilling your potential…well, I just seem to be getting a bit confused here."

"Yeah, I know; I also find it confusing sometimes. I imagine that if you are someone who is fully conscious and in the here now, which would probably mean that you're 'enlightened', you no longer have any desires, or dreams, or longings and are fulfilled.

But for the rest of us, if you put acceptance against fighting instead of longing, then maybe it gets a bit clearer?" Stella suggested.

"You think so?"

"Yes, or at least I hope so. Maybe it's like comparing apples with pears, but let's see if we can find an example."

"That could make it clearer. Anything coming to mind?"

"Ok, maybe this could work. Say, for example, that you're on your way to see someone you long to see, but get a flat tyre. Instead of going on and on about the injustice of getting a flat tyre at that moment, being in a hurry, wasting a lot of energy on brooding and probably becoming irritated, you could just say, 'A flat tyre', or maybe even add 'shit!', but then say, 'Okay, what should I do?' and use the energy to do something about it, like change wheels or call for help."

"Okay, that does make it clearer, I think. Although perhaps not so much in terms of longings and desires, if I may say so, but still taking the action needed to get to see the longed for friend. Ok; for now." I looked at her and smiled. "In any case, as we discussed some time ago, being here now may include planning and acting to make a longing or desire materialise in the future. Actually, it might even be necessary sometimes."

"When you wish upon a star...tralalalalalala! Stella teased. "No, sorry, of course. Kind of." We both laughed.

That theme of desires, longings, acceptance and fighting, lingered with me for some time. I was beginning to see that in a way both desires and

221

longings mean that what is here now is not perceived as fulfilling, hence we fight with reality and want something else, something more. That said; if I were fully here now and accept what is, could I not have a longing for something anyway?

The metaphor of comparing apples to pears also came back to me more than once. I could not help but surrender to my limitations and realise that I am here now, enjoying the present as much as I can. I do sometimes try to plan what I would like to do in the future and what I need to do to make it happen, and that is alright. Given that, it may be helpful to see to it to find myself now here, rather than lose myself in nowhere. Like some friends often say: "No worries mate".

Chapter 24

Stella Strips a Long Story Short and Makes Her Debut

Despite all our defences
And different pretences
If we really look and don't go astray
We can see through like an x-ray
What's moving in ourselves and in the other
And choose to lovingly bother
Neither for nor against
But with

"So how is it going?"

"How's what going?"

"Your writing."

"Oh...did you have to ask that? I was almost hoping you wouldn't bring that up again, or had forgotten."

Apparently I had been optimistic.

"How could I forget? I'm curious! Did you at least put something together for the readers' contest in that magazine I gave you?"

Carl had given me a women's magazine a couple of weeks before. I was so surprised at the time that I even missed the opportunity to tease him about reading that kind of magazine.

"You mean that frivolous 'the woman in you talking' thing?"

"That's the one," Carl confirmed.

"Don't you think that was a bit over the top to start with?"

"No, I obviously don't." He laughed. "I cannot think of why it should be, at least not for you, and does it really matter where you start? Moreover, there was a word limit, which I would suspect could make it feasible, at least time-wise."

He really could be persistent.

"No, I guess you're right, and I guess it doesn't," I conceded.

"And I'm still waiting for the answer?"

"Actually, I did manage to find the time to put a little something together."

"Great! May I read it soon?" Carl asked with anticipation.

"Well, if you really want to; that could actually happen sooner rather than later."

"It could?"

"Yes, believe it or not. The deadline is the day after tomorrow, so I brought a copy with me in case you raised the subject. I would like your opinion before I decide to send it in."

"What if I hadn't brought it up – and if I don't happen to like it? Would you send it anyway?"

"I don't know…but I think so."

"Good." Carl looked pleased.

"You know; this is the first time since school that someone else will have read what I've written; I mean letters, of course, but that's different and meant for the one reading. In university, it was more scientific and work reports are factual; this is more personal, even though it is not, if you understand what I mean."

"Yes, I think I do. Please, may I read it now?"

I lifted the printout from my bag and handed it to him.

"Promise me you will be honest and say what you really think when you've read it? And please be nice…"

"Thank you. Ok, I promise I'll be honest. And I'm sure nice will go with it too."

Carl started reading and I tried to enjoy my coffee. I looked around at people, wrote to-do lists, went to the ladies' toilet and became increasingly more nervous. The subject too felt quite embarrassing, but like he had said, why not throw myself in, make a jump-start and see what comes with it? So I did. He held the first result in his hands. I closed my eyes and monitored my breathing for a while, then had the story running in the back of my mind.

Hello my dear,

I met Amy the other day. It's simply incredible how she tries to avoid me. Comes up with this and that. I bet she'll soon start cleaning cupboards too.

Hellooo!! I'm here!! I have always been here and always will be here. Often ignored, secluded, but here. Without any nickname and with my fiery, red energy, with my warm, soft, protecting flesh. Much alone, sometimes lonely and longing for visits, to show that I exist, even if it has been so abandoned here for so long that I would barely remember how to behave should the occasion occur. Hell no, it has to be when the occasion occurs. Even though pretty shut down, I couldn't escape from The Big System Crash. Dry, sensitive, shy, but inside also voluptuous, passionate, pulsating, juicy. Like in that dream a while ago. I could hardly tell whether it was for real or not. Not. But so bloody good! Like an appetiser for the real thing – or most likely better. I wonder who he was?

The ones who have been here and have been good are few, and preferably someone new, rather than impossible old stories.

She did actually buy one of those pets on the Internet. Progress, I thought. Like in 'Sex and the City', but here all similarities cease. It has visited a few times, although somehow not for real. It is as if she is afraid of what would happen, even though it's only her and me. A little warming up sometimes, then: "No. Enough is enough." In principle, all of adult life so far has been like that. Except a few years a long time ago.

I don't get it that she doesn't get it, doesn't realise, that by secluding me she is also rejecting a part of her femininity, energy, joy, life; all that she says she is longing for. The femininity she largely feels she is lacking; I could be a key! And supposedly there is no flipside to this coin. Maybe after all, slowly, slowly, something has started happening. Maybe she is gradually beginning to see, to feel, to dare, to play. Torn between the whore and the Madonna, not wanting to be neither one or the other, and getting stuck in the pre-pubescent girl limbo.

But there in between, between the whore and the Madonna, the Woman actually is. That is where I want to be; that is where I am. If she only dares to start saying 'Yes!' to me, to her woman, to her energy. And she – we – have been there sniffing a little bit the last few years. She has had moments when she has felt her power, her joy, has let the hips swing and just vibrated

226

with exuberant, luscious energy. Then the block has hit again. Back to the old, just as some playing, some excitement, started happening.

Yet sometimes...sometimes she's in, here, where we are; sometimes she does let sensuality wake up, does let longing wake up. Feeling the wind in her face, on her skin, feeling the soft skin, touch, flavours, fragrances, the consistency of food, baking, cooking, creating, laughing, crying; a few more feminine clothes, a little more feminine, a little more alive. A woman. I love it! She loves it! Why is she so afraid then? Why this seriousness? Why this potential denial of what is life, of what is human, albeit sometimes animalistic? It seems to run deep, hard. The patriarchy's control over women? Priests' control over people and particularly women? Mother's and father's fear of what others might say; grandchildren too soon? Does it matter? Here and now it shouldn't have to be that way, should it? Life is too short not to be lived, not to be enjoyed. And then I matter. Much as it would seem. At least according to some.

At the same time, it's not only me she has denied; the whole body has got its share – or the opposite. The years when she almost didn't eat, literally denying herself nourishment, life. Her periods stopped, the breasts shrunk. The budding woman was cut off. Frozen, eventually starting to defrost. I can sometimes feel grief, also her grief, for all that we may have missed on the way, or maybe not. Perhaps the sorrow and the tears melt the frozenness. If so, what happens when the tears have gone? Sometimes a kind of lust for revenge comes. I can, I want to, I will! What is it that makes our bodies and sex so ambiguous? After all, everybody has one and we're born naked. Few things are perceived as shameful as the naked body; few things are so desirable as the 'perfect' naked body, maybe subtly covered here and there. And isn't 'perfect' actually boring, predictable, lifeless? She has never really seen her body, hasn't liked it, much less really felt that it could be desirable. Ok, she is starting to feel it a little – and to feel me. To feel gratitude for it, despite – or maybe because of – some bodily challenges; to feel herself in it, accept it, like it. To like me. A new bud on its way to bursting and this time it will – we will – blossom.

I don't know what this flower will look like, but it will be beautiful. All flowers are so fabulously beautiful if you really look at them, aren't they? That's the way it is with us too. Everybody has his or her place. So do I. I have the right to take space. She has the right to take space. Her space. I just wish she would do it soon, now! Just do it! I used to think that I didn't like her, that she betrayed me, so I have in some sense betrayed her back, but now I just feel compassion and love, a longing for reconciliation. She is me, I am her. No matter what, when, or how.

I'm longing to explore, to play with creativity, sensuality, sexuality, life. I'm longing to feel the pulse, to get hot, to desire, to feel desired, and filled with passion. A passion flower! And love and relaxation therewith. To be enjoyed.

Love,
Thea

"Stella…"

"Yes?" I opened my eyes and looked at him.

"I'm happy you made the font size so big."

"What?"

"You heard me." He smiled and gave me that mischievous look. "You know; I've reached that age when I suddenly understand the importance of font size to legibility."

"If I had something hard I'd throw it at you! I'll take the bag."

I grabbed my handbag and made a symbolic move as to throw it on him over the table. He ducked and raised an arm as to protect himself, laughing. I could not but laugh, too.

"I'm sorry, I couldn't help it since I could feel a certain tension in the air."

"Yes, I bet you could; you kind, caring friend. Be my guest, just prolong the agony I'm going through."

"Yeah, well you know your Nietzsche and his Zarathustra, don't you? The part where what doesn't kill you makes you stronger," Carl teased.

"Like I said, you're so sweet and I'm so strong."

We both laughed again.

"You are. Among other things."

"Yeah…and right now strong enough to feel very vulnerable, to tell you the truth."

"I get it and, seriously, I'm honoured."

"Come on, and ok, I'm glad, but please! You have no idea how this is making me nervous," I confessed.

"Oh yeah? This might come as a surprise to you, but you're making it kind of obvious." Carl smiled, and looked at me. "Ok, I'll announce my verdict."

He hesitated theatrically before he went on.

"I really like this. As strange as it may sound coming from me as a man, I think it says a lot about many women's situation; your strength and vulnerability and I do hope you'll send it to that magazine. And I also hope you will continue writing."

"You're not just being nice now?"

"No, I'm honest, and if that goes together with nice, then all the better."

"Thank you. I'm relieved." I took a deep breath. "I must admit I like writing fiction and stuff, but so far it's like I can't just sit down and write on command so-to-speak. It happens more often when a phrase, or sentence, or something comes to me, pops up – and stays with me – then it flows and grows in its own way for a while. Until it doesn't." I described my experiences so far in this area.

"That sounds good enough to me and I hope those sentences will keep coming. I have a feeling they will." Carl encouraged. "By the way, would you say you recognise yourself in this?"

"Of course, there are parts where I've used my experiences and also others' as a starting point, then I just allow the hands to move on the keyboard. It's funny, one might think that as a writer I would decide what a character will say or do, but more often than not I actually am surprised by what comes, what he or she says or does. Maybe I could challenge you to write a 'the man-in-you thing'?"

"Oh no, but since you mention it, that could be another challenge for you," Carl retorted.

"I'm not a man." I smiled.

"No, obviously you are not, but we all have both and you and I both know, women have been known to write about men and vice versa."

"Ha, ha, that's a canny observation."

"And you can as always use a writer's freedom, like you did already in this," Carl stated.

"For sure. No promises, but thank you for the suggestion. If I do go ahead with it, maybe I could get some inspiration from you, should I get stuck?"

"If you think I could contribute, I would be happy to," Carl laughed.

"Good."

"Now you'd better see to it that you put this one in the mail tomorrow, or even better, tonight."

"If you say so, I will."

"Well, please, not because I say so, but because you want to."

"Ok."

"And promise me that even if you don't win, you won't let that put you off and keep on writing anyway."

"Win??" I laughed and almost choked on my coffee. "Are you crazy?"

"Well, if you take part in a competition, there's a part of you that would like to win, isn't there? Not every participant can win and certainly it cannot be expected to happen every time." Carl was being realistic.

"Hmmm…to be honest, you've got a point there. And there are different kinds of victories, aren't there? Winning a competition of course is an obvious one, but when it comes to this writing thing, it would be incredibly beautiful to me if some people at least would enjoy reading what I write and find that it gives something to them, like it gives me something to write it. That would be more important than winning any contest, even though that would probably help make people curious."

"Of course. In the same way, it could feel like a victory to us, if we manage to do something we thought we couldn't do previously, or wouldn't dare to do, like you with writing and sending in this short story."

"Yes. And if something happens to us, like a disease, or accident, or something that affects our abilities, being able to do everyday things, which we took for granted, can feel like a victory."

"Yes, it is kind of humbling to remind oneself about things like that every now and then, isn't it?"

"It is. And I will send my little story in. After that, we can only wait and see what happens." I had made my mind up.

"Yes! You will at least have a chance to win then." Carl smiled.

"Ha, ha, like buying a lottery ticket you mean?"

"Ha, ha, yes, something like that."

"Thank you for your support. I might go and buy a lottery ticket as well."

"Since we're talking about it, let's go and do that. I'll buy one too and maybe we should also buy one together. I feel lucky."

Carl stood up, and I put my things together so we could leave.

"Yes, let's do that. But you know, I already feel like I've won big time." I looked at him. He looked back at me, and smiled.

"Me too actually. We both have, haven't we?"

Although writing a piece and placing it under public scrutiny was new to me, the feeling of being a winner was not. Admittedly, for the sake of balance, neither was the feeling sometimes of being a loser. However, life as such, friends, the body, the beauty of nature, music and so much else, often fill me with awe and a feeling of being incredibly fortunate. And I am.

Chapter 25

Carl Keeps His Real Estate Dreams and Stands His Ground with Stella

Now it is soon
Soon it will be now
- And now is!

"Do you still have dreams?" Stella asked.

"That's an interesting question. Why shouldn't I? Of course I do, we all do; it's just that we don't always remember them. You know that."

"Of course, sorry, I didn't mean dreams when you sleep. I meant dreams or wishes, like something you'd like to become or do, or somewhere you'd like to go, or whatever you might come up with?"

I began wondering where Stella was heading with this. We had touched on a subject including dreams not long ago; rather recently, since I remembered it.

"Ok, dreams...yes, I'd say I do, both big and small; 'dreams' is quite a wide concept," I replied.

"Absolutely, and you can start wherever you like. I remember you dreaming or rather fantasising about becoming a millionaire, which now I would interpret as a wish to become financially independent, and becoming a world champion in racket-ball or what was it?" Stella reminded me of some of my, perhaps, more grandiose tendencies.

"Hey, you just added a couple of things to my list." I smiled.

"Glad to be of service," Stella laughed.

234

"I bet. Well, on the list there is also world peace, no more famine, a cure for all diseases, healthy children and family." I realised I was probably provoking her a bit.

"Ok, ok…I get it. You're very noble, but if we stick to your personal life?"

"Hmm, between us, I still dream about building a house at the waterfront on my favourite island," I revealed.

"Did you manage to get hold of the land you once showed me?" Stella again proved her good memory.

"Not yet, but you never know."

"I'll keep my fingers crossed. It's a beautiful place. Do you have some plans drawn up, or some ideas sketched?"

"I have, and every now and then I have a look at them, or go out there and just sit and picture it all in front of me. I listen to the sounds of the trees, the sea, sense the sweetness and the saltiness in the air, admire the scenery, imagine the house and think about what kind of garden I'd like to have there."

I looked out of the window as if I would see it all out there.

"Mmmm…wonderful. Did you also contact the owner? If you applied, do you think you would get a permit to build? Sorry, I sound like an interrogation leader," Stella apologised.

"Don't worry; I appreciate your keen interest. It would probably be ok to build, since there is already a small old barn on the land."

"You'd better have that checked out before you make an offer or anything," Stella advised.

"Yes, you're right, I do. Strangely enough, I keep postponing it; it is as if I'm afraid of getting a 'no' and losing the dream." I just realised it as I heard myself saying it.

"I was just going to ask what you think is holding you back? I think I understand that feeling; that's probably the underlying reason why I never entered medical school, or at least part of the reason."

"Tell me," I urged.

"Well, what or who would I be if my dream turned out to be a foolish illusion; turned out to be a disappointment? In addition, further down the line, what if a patient died because of a mistake I made?"

"Ha, someone who went to law school instead? And for the record, of all the people I know, you are probably the one least likely to make such a fatal mistake."

"Yeah, right, you never know though, but thanks anyway."

"And now, how about you, Stella; what are your dreams these days?"

"Actually, I don't know if I have any dreams any more. Of course, I could picture myself going on a dream holiday to a luxurious resort in the Maldives, Seychelles or the Caribbean, or somewhere similar with blue skies, turquoise water and white sand."

"That sounds perfect for you, since you love swimming, snorkelling, diving and sunbathing..." Irony was sometimes too tempting to me.

"It does, doesn't it? Apparently, I didn't think of those little details. I was thinking more of a beautiful view from under a parasol." Stella smiled.

"Nothing wrong with that; at least not if you add a passionate lover following and satisfying all your desires...or maybe a pile of good books." I could not help but tease Stella a little more.

"Now we're talking…and you have me blushing."

"I like that." I did.

"Hmm…my blushing, or the thought of me and my pile of books?" Stella asked and we both laughed.

I thought that we would need to watch out or we would be in danger of becoming out-dated and hopelessly old-fashioned. A Kindle or iPad filled with e-books had become the modern version of a pile of books, and neither of us brought that up, even though it would make the luggage lighter. I let that thought pass and looked at her.

"Both! So, anything else? Think big!"

"Ha, ha, I seem to be as much into big thinking as I am into small talking. Well, when I was a young girl, I used to fantasise about becoming a doctor as I said, meeting an attractive, intelligent man, having two or perhaps three kids, a successful career, a nice house; you know, the package with a gilded touch."

"And now?"

"Now, obviously, none of that has happened or will, and I cannot really say that something else – other dreams – have taken its place. Even if I could come up with what could be called dreams, like a flat with a sea-facing terrace, somewhere with a temperate climate, or writing a best-selling novel, or whatever…I can't really feel it as a driving force." Stella stated and shrugged.

"Is that good or bad? And I wonder why you just ruled out the attractive, intelligent man?" I asked.

"You tell me; I don't know. Apparently, he is not a priority; maybe it's not an unfulfilled need or desire anymore." She smiled. "It's just that my life has taken a different turn and, most of the time, I like where I am. A lot."

"Yes, that sounds good. You don't seem to be regretful or bitter to me – quite the opposite. And I've always been a very good judge of character you know!"

"Sure darling." Stella smiled.

"Seriously, I mean it; you don't seem bitter or even disillusioned for that matter."

"Good, and I usually don't feel bitter. Why should I? Maybe a bit disillusioned sometimes."

We both laughed again.

"Well, who isn't?"

"And by the way, where did that come from?" She gave me a probing eye.

"What?"

"The idea of bitterness – or possibly non-bitterness?"

"Frankly, I don't know…probably just my ideas and projections," I admitted.

"Well, what isn't, for all of us? Anyway, it doesn't matter. So, now that we agree that I'm not bitter…" She looked at me, made a face then smiled. "Let's say I'm usually happily un-normal, and maybe un-normally happy too, instead of normally un-happy." She blinked.

"Ha, ha, yes, that's already something!"

"Nevertheless, there have of course been moments of sadness and even questioning."

"Sorry, but sadness is pretty normal. As is questioning," I interrupted, emitting a theatrical sigh.

"Really?" She pretended to sound surprised. "Shit, there goes my cover-up."

"Got you! Life is a bitch sometimes…and then we die."

"Bugger!"

"So, Stella, what is it you've questioned or felt sad about?"

"Oh...different things, like if I'm really true to myself; if I've lost something, if I no longer have dreams, or if I am actually just accepting what is and happily living in the moment."

"Well, that is something only you would know. I guess whether you would feel regret or not for something not happening and you could have done something about it could be a hint. So what happened to that thought – was it a dream or what that you had about actually writing a novel?"

"Oh, you remember that one too."

"Of course. And you just gave it as an example."

"You're right. I don't know; maybe that's part of my lost illusions, or maybe an outcome of my inner critic, or was a sign of hubris. Or maybe it will happen, just not yet," Stella reflected.

"But you still keep up with the writing, at least for yourself, don't you? And you did write that short story."

"Yes, I did and I do. Well, perhaps not on a regular basis, because it comes and goes, but yes, it is an outlet for me; like a pondering, a watching in writing. Things often become clearer when I put them on paper. Thoughts, emotions, mind-fuck, ideas, insights and fantasies. Sometimes it's just like an overflow, something that wants to find an expression and sometimes a story presents itself; at times by way of a poem, at other times less structured – like free word embroidery, or whatever. I'm surprised you came back to this and still listen."

"I really think you should tell that inner critic of yours to go and have a rest, you know. I think you have a lot to share that would also mean something to other people, including me."

"You do?"

"Yes!"

"Thank you. As limiting and sneaky as that critic is, it sometimes has a kind of grandiosity, which he, or she, or they use in several ways. One is somehow inverted: how big doesn't he fear me to be if I need all those rules? And how 'perfect' must I not be to obey all of them? Another is to use it against me: how grandiose am I to think that I could do this or that, like for instance write a novel that will be published, or even worse, publish it myself?"

"For heaven's sake, it is about bloody time you give yourself a break and some time to do things like writing and see what comes. If you can't defend against those critical, judging voices in one way or the other, please call me!" Perhaps this was a bit blunt, but I felt it needed to be said and whatever works, works.

"You're sweet." No doubt Stella was embarrassed.

"Maybe I am, but I didn't intend to be sweet; this is to make you see things and yourself the way you deserve, and so the rest of us for that matter could get to enjoy it. I would be honoured if you would let me read your first manuscript, or whatever you'd like to call it, as you allowed me to read your short story."

"I'm happy to have my first reader then, whenever it happens. That would be a beautiful gift and inspiration, thank you. I'll try." Stella affirmed.

"Skip 'try' and just do it. If not now, when? Just to remind you, more than once I've heard you say that life is here now and we have no idea about tomorrow. What's the worst that can happen? Except regret if you don't. You just keep on breathing and be ready when inspiration hits and creativity flows. I probably don't have to point out to you, of all people, the connection between breathing and 'in-spiration', do I? Stella gave me a broad smile. "I'll just be on your case, and that's a promise."

I would not let her hide behind excuses and cop out on this one.

"We're quite a team, aren't we?" Stella said.

"Oh yes, and there's no way you will get rid of me, since I am you and you are me. And finally we seem to get along quite well together."

"Yes. The odds of this happening would have been pretty high for a while, wouldn't they?" Stella remarked.

"What would you say; a big surprise or inevitable?" I asked.

"Hmmm…whatever; it doesn't really matter, does it? Thank you for coming today, before and later. I really appreciate it, and your masculine energy. I really appreciate you. In fact, I love you Carl."

"You're a wonderful woman Stella. I love you too."

Suddenly there was the sound of languishing strings in the loudspeakers, like in a movie. Obviously, one could say the director had done a diligent job. Not that this was a particularly romantic moment, but most certainly love was in the air. We had travelled some distance, Stella and I; from being colleagues, lovers, partners, separated, to being close, caring, loving friends. Friends that can be honest, open, straight and vulnerable with each other. Looking back, strangely enough it did not feel like we had had that the first round and now we did. Who knows about tomorrow?

241

Chapter 26

Stella in Her Way Advocates That Easy is Right, Right is Easy

Every moment
A piece of art
Breathing
In the beauty
Until no more

It was one of those lazy Sundays, albeit on a Tuesday. I had nothing planned, went from here to there, coming up with a thousand and one little things I ought to do, but getting nothing done and starting to feel guilty about wasting precious time, when the phone rang – saved by the bell! It was Carl.

"Pronto!"

"Hi Stella! Practising your Italian, are you?"

"Si, I just reached the advanced level."

"I bet. You're a bit slow though."

"I'm not three anymore."

"Thank goodness for that! Listen; as you know I'll be away for some time, so I was wondering if you would mind booking an afternoon for us when I get back? If you'll be around, that is?"

"Oh Carl, I love you – us – and the way we have to make life complicated."

"I hear your smile Stella. I know, but I guess a part of me is afraid that we'll drift apart again, and Skype and chats and texts and whatever, however good and helpful they might be, are not like a come-together in real life. And that part of me also wants to know that as far as we are concerned, we have a come-together planned. That's actually not so complicated, is it?"

"Maybe we're not three but five again. Yes, please, let's make complicated easy and easy complicated and meet on the Wednesday after you come home – usual place, usual time, alright? Would that be ok with you?"

"It would. I'll add it to my iPhone calendar and send it to yours."

"Great, thank you Carl. You know, as absurd as it may sound, I sometimes wonder…"

"What?"

"When is it you come home?" I asked, giggling.

"Oh you're such a tease! On the Saturday before we meet; ha, ha."

"Sweet revenge! No worries, I know, but please let me know should you change your plans."

"Of course," Carl assured. "And the same goes for you."

"Yes. Anyway, what I meant was that many of us have this habit of making such a fuss of life, often making things complicated, and who knows, we might actually just be living in someone else's dream."

"Ouch, now, that was a nice see-you-soon gift. Please let's have that subject on the table the next time we meet – unless that someone has woken up by then. And by the way, I know I'm living my dream, ha, ha!"

"I bet you do – and I do too!"

The End.

To be continued…

243

Epilogue

I woke up, not really wanting to open my eyes and get going, but to stay in this space between wakefulness and sleep. I could feel my head and cheek resting on the pillow, one hand holding the duvet, the other lying on the side of my chest, the right side of the body enjoying the soft support of the mattress, legs halfway bent, one foot out. I usually sleep on my side; sometimes the left, sometimes the right. Now...slowly...sleep was giving way to awakening.

I moved my hands, stretched my body and rolled to the back. I wiped the sleep away from the corners of my eyes, opened them, blinked a couple of times and looked around my bedroom at the white ceiling, the familiar pictures on the walls, the fireplace, the armchair with some of my previous day's clothes on it, the chest of drawers, the lilac linen curtains and the flowers on the windowsill casting some shadows.

The thought that I had to call Carl and Stella and invite them to dinner soon flashed through my head, eliciting happy feelings about sharing an evening with such dear friends. Then it struck me: I did not know a Carl or Stella. It was all in a dream, yet so intense and with such detail, that I was sure it must have been real. I even took my phone to check the contacts. No Carl. No Stella.

Later on, I met with and talked to a deeply loved friend; a real one, Vita, and shared my dream and morning with her. I told her I was afraid I might be going crazy; that dream was so real, yet it was nothing but a movie from the unconscious, an illusion. Could it be that our lives that we believe are so real are just an illusion too; a movie on a screen vaster than ours?

Obviously our minds have a tendency to run their own movies, usually based upon conditioning, ideas, experiences, and who knows what, imprinted in us from very early on; maybe even before us.

Vita looked at me for a while, letting what I had just said sink in. Then she asked me how I felt in the dream and when I woke up. I closed my eyes and recalled how I felt. Opening my eyes again, I shared with her that, strangely, I had the sensation of feeling joyous, genuine and alive with both of them, and when I woke up and realised I could not call them, I missed them and felt sad.

My eyes met Vita's and rested for a while. After some moments, Vita said that it sounded to her like I would not have to miss them; that they probably could be seen as reflections of my inner male and female sides. She then asked whether that made any sense to me. A surprising number of thoughts ran through my mind. Could it really be? How come it felt so real, that they felt like two friends, each with their own lives? All this focus that so many of us put on outer polarities; could that be mirroring our inner polarities and vice versa?

Trying to solve that would probably take forever and a day, hence it would be better just to dissolve into it. I looked at Vita and slowly answered that I did not know if I would agree to it literally making sense, but...yes, I thought it could be one possibility. She continued by stating that the fact that I felt good with both of them could be a sign that I had actually made friends with myself and felt good about myself. Her observation puzzled me a bit, but made me happy.

"Seriously? For real?"

"Seriously. For real," she replied, with a gleam in her eye, adding that only I would know.

We both cracked up laughing until we cried, followed by silence and relaxation. Friends, alone together.

Dancing without music
Singing without voice
Celebrating for no reason
Like butterflies in the lavender
Living is every reason

Acknowledgements

To begin with, my gratitude turns to you who have read this story all the way to here, as well as to you who have arrived at this page, perhaps without reading or browsing the prior ones. My wish is that you have gained something worthwhile out of it.

However, as a background to this beginning, my gratitude also goes to life for allowing me to enter this body, to my parents for having me, for bringing me up, for giving me love and support – and to them, my brother and his family for bearing with me. I thank this body too, the temple that houses me, that carries me around, that is such a generous teacher and guide – in spite of me not often being a very attentive listener. Together we have been travelling on outer and inner journeys for some time now and hopefully will continue doing so for much longer.

These journeys have given me the privilege of meeting so many dear friends and people, who all give me such a variety of experiences that have brought me to where I am today, and to this story.

There are also friends that I feel I want to mention here, since your loving support in various ways gave me the courage to go through and play with this venture, even though my love and gratitude to you are beyond words: Dwari, Devapath, Shunyo, Agni, Agyana and last, but not least, Osho, a man and master I never got to meet in these our bodies, but whom, nevertheless, I am touched and inspired by, and keep on meeting again and again. You are all so precious to me.

How it all happened eludes me, yet I love this mystery and bow down to all of you who take part in it, earlier, now and later. Thank you.

Appendix

Suggested reading:

Hellinger, Bert; Love's Hidden Symmetry
www.hellinger.com

Osho; The Diamond Sutra
Osho; The Discipline of Transcendence
Osho; Guida Spirituale
Osho; Intimacy – Trusting Oneself and the Other
Osho; Meditation – The First and Last Freedom
Osho; Tantra: The Supreme Understanding
Osho; Unio Mystica
www.osho.com

Ma Prem Shunyo; My Diamond Days with Osho